KASH

ARMY RANGERS SPECIAL OPS

SUSIE MCIVER

KASH

ARMY RANGERS SPECIAL OPS: BOOK ONE

AUTHOR
SUSIE MCIVER

1

KASH

Damn, I'm tired. I ran my fingers through my hair—
Home sweet home. I couldn't wait to shower and crawl into
my bed. I needed twelve hours of sleep but could settle for
at least six. I looked around my house before letting Max out
the back door. Max did well on this trip, so I promised him a
steak dinner. He caught one of the shooters before the guy
shot one of us. I was thankful we made it back safe from
Afghanistan. I hated going to that place, but I would keep
going until we had everyone out of there.

This time, we were able to rescue thirty Americans. Now,
hopefully, I'll have some time to rest before we go again. I
couldn't believe how close we came to not getting out of
there. All I want now is a shower, a bed, and nothing else.
Why the hell am I talking to myself? That just goes to show
that I need my rest.

I abruptly sat up in bed, my mind racing with questions.
What was that noise? Was it screaming? Did someone need help?
Damn it, I had barely managed to fall asleep. Were those
kids I could hear? Where was all that commotion coming
from? I stopped to listen and glanced at the clock; it read ten

a.m. If I didn't address that noise, I'd never get any sleep. Where the hell were those kids?

Throwing off the covers, I rushed out to the backyard, only to realize I was completely naked. Damn. I hurried back inside and grabbed a pair of sweatpants from the dryer, letting out a yelp of pain as I accidentally hit my toe.

I glanced at the box of books that had been sitting there for six months. I rubbed my stiff neck, thinking I needed a massage. One day, I'd go through those books. They had belonged to my dad, who was a passionate reader, and my mom had given them to me, saying I would read them. However, I never seemed to have time for anything these days.

As I opened the back door, the noise grew louder. I looked over the fence and couldn't believe what I saw. Kids were everywhere, and my massive German Shepherd was running back and forth, chasing the basketball while the boys played. When did that basketball hoop get there?

Among the children, a baby girl rolled around in a walker, she was playing with Max, my ferocious guard dog, who always growled at anyone who came around my place. He licked the baby's face, so he could hear her giggling. 'I've never seen him play with kids before,' I mumbled under my breath.

Then, I noticed a woman's backside in the air, and my body betrayed me by instantly becoming aroused. It been a while since I've had sex, and that curvy figure was damn enticing. She wore blue cutoffs and a pink tank top, with a thick braid cascading over her shoulder as she tended to a garden. When the heck was that container garden been set up? Hell, I'd only been gone six weeks.

All I could see was the back of her, so why was I getting so damn turned on? I hoped my mom hadn't rent the house to someone with children. The last couple who rented the place was old and quiet. My number one rule had always been no kids, they are always noisy and messy.

I HAD BOUGHT this house next door to prevent noisy neighbors from moving in. If my mom had rented it to someone with kids, then she would have to un-rent it. I'm going to call her and remind her of the rules. I pushed open the gate and walked over to their side of the backyard.

"Excuse me, did you rent this house, or are you visiting the tenant?" I inquired, hoping they were just visiting their grandma.

It appeared she was ignoring me, continuing to work in the garden. "Is she ignoring me?" I muttered. It seemed she was indeed ignoring me, and I wasn't used to being disregarded like that.

"We just moved in last month," a young teenage boy said, "is this your dog? He's awesome. He wanted to play with us. I hope you don't mind that I opened the gate for him so he could come over."

Their mother was awfully rude, ignoring my question and letting the kid answer for her. "I was talking to your mother."

"Emily isn't our mom; she's our sister. Hang on," a young teenage boy named Jason replied before tapping Emily on the shoulder.

❧

I STOOD UP, looked at my brother, and smiled. I loved my siblings so much. The kids had too much heartache. It was so hard for them to lose both parents at the same time.

"Emily, this man wants to talk to you," Jason told her, using sign language.

I was taken aback when I turned around to face the man in question. "Wow!" That was the only word that crossed my mind. He was incredibly handsome, and he wanted to talk to me. He wasn't wearing a shirt, and his sweatpants hung low on his hips. I couldn't spot an ounce of fat on him; he was all muscle. Barefoot and with no visible underclothes, he looked quite enticing. I could even see where his hairline disappeared into his sweats. Suddenly, I felt my nipples harden, and I glanced down, realizing that I had forgotten to put on a bra. My face flushed, and I was sure it was as red as a fire truck.

Finally, I raised my eyes to his face, and my breath hitched. He had the longest, dark lashes and the sexiest blue eyes I had ever seen. As I gawked at him, I sucked in a breath. I was sure my mouth hung open. I couldn't help it; this half-naked man was beautiful, and I think I drooled. I looked at Jason, who signed that the guy lived next door.

"How can I help you?" I asked, and I could tell he was surprised I spoke normally. Most people assumed I couldn't speak normally either because I couldn't hear well. However, my hearing had only started when I was ten years old.

I ALMOST TRIPPED on my own feet when she looked at me. I took in my fill and realized how rude I was being, but I wasn't expecting that beautiful smile. I ran my hand through my hair. I knew that probably made it stand up worse. I remembered I went to sleep with it wet, so I knew it was a mess. I needed another haircut.

Damn it, Kash, leave your damn hair alone. She'll think you're weird. I eased my hand down and cleared my throat. I looked around. Where did all the flowers come from? Did she plant all of this?

"I live next door. I didn't get to bed until a couple of hours ago. So, I'd like to get some sleep. But the noise from the kids woke me up."

I waited for her to ask the kids to quiet down or something, but to my surprise, she chuckled.

A chuckle escaped her again before she replied to me, "I'm sorry, I'll tell them they can't play basketball until..." She paused and looked at me. "What time works for you?"

I found myself locked in her beautiful gaze, unable to look away, even though her eyes seemed to be laughing at me.. "I'm not usually up all night; I'm not a night owl or anything like that. But I didn't get in until this morning. I've been out of the country for over a month. By the way, how did you get my dog to come over here?"

"OH, he kept trying to get over the fence so he could play with the kids. I was going to suggest, if you're okay with it, that we can leave the gate open, and he can play with the kids whenever he wants ."

I couldn't believe what I was hearing. Was she out of her mind? The last thing I needed was a neighbor with five kids.

"That's not going to happen. Max is a dangerous dog; he's trained as an attack dog, for Christ's sake. He apprehends criminals and holds them until I call him off. He doesn't play with kids. He's part of a Special Ops team. I don't want the gate left open. I value my privacy."

"Wow, did you hear that, kids? Max is the dog's name and works with the Special Ops team. He must be an Army

Ranger. Right? Of course, I don't know what your privacy has to do with your dog visiting us. Unless you're afraid, Max will spill your secrets. Just kidding," she said with a grin, seemingly not taking me seriously.

I NARROWED my eyes as I looked at her. "Yes, Army Rangers. I feel like you misunderstood me. I meant I want the gate kept shut. That is what has to do with my privacy. I built Max a dog run; this gate ensures we both have privacy.

"I UNDERSTAND. My name is Emily Jones. These four are my brothers, Jason, Tommy, Brian, and Mikey, and this sweet baby girl is our sister, Kelsey. I'm sorry the kids woke you up. Are you going to stay up? If you are, the boys can keep playing. If not, we'll go inside or to the park."

I watched her turn to the boys, and they groaned loudly. She could tell I heard their groans as well, and I couldn't hide the frown on my face. Kids needed to be outside playing, not be cooped up indoors when the sun was shining. I was starting to feel guilty.

I LOOKED AT EMILY AGAIN. I relented because I didn't want to be known as the neighborhood grouch. "I'll stay up." The boys erupted in cheers throwing their fists in the air. Then they started playing again. I looked down at the baby; she was clapping her little hands together.

I mumbled something under my breath about bratty kids as I turned to head back to my place, but Emily's voice stopped me. Her voice was like hot, sweet Tennessee whiskey, seductive and sexy. It was as if her voice had the smoothness of buttery rum. She had me aroused once again.

"I can't hear you if you aren't looking at me. I lost my hearing aids when I fell while a car nearly ran me over on the sidewalk. When I fell, my hearing aids fell out. So please talk to me when we're facing each other."

I turned back around to talk to Emily. "Of course, I'm sorry."

After we finished talking I went back to my house, the first thing I did was call my mother. "Hello, darling. Are you home?"

"THAT'S NOT GOING to work, Mom. You know I don't want kids living next door to me. I've only had three hours of sleep in three days because of the noise coming from the rental woke me up. You'll have to give them notice to find another place to live. You can even refund them for this month."

"Kash, darling, I can't do that. These kids have been through hell. They lost their parents in a horrible freak accident on the freeway."

"Come on, Mom. That's emotional blackmail. I have my rules, and you're breaking them."

"It's not a matter of blackmailing you, my darling. I just think it would be too much for that poor girl to handle. Emily is their older sister from their father's first marriage and she's doing everything she can for those kids."

Emily moved back from Colorado to care for her siblings after quitting a good job, so they could continue attending their school. She couldn't afford the payments on their home, and with all the bills piling up, she had to sell the family home to settle their debts. I'm... we are all the help she has. What if I talk to Emily about keeping the noise down?"

"Mom, I don't want to know their backstory. I'm sorry they lost their parents; it's something no child should ever go through. But you know I value my privacy. The kids are already talking about leaving the gate open so Max can come and go as he pleases. Wait, did you just chuckle?"

"No..." I could tell she was lying. "I'll speak to Emily. Please be gentle with the children's feelings. I know you haven't been around kids much, but please don't scold them."

"Mom, I'm not Scrooge. I won't even be mean to them, nor will I intentionally hurt their feelings. How do you know so much about them? Wait! Why would you think I would yell at them?"

"I'm sorry I said that. Of course, you wouldn't yell at them. Your dad and Bill, their father, were Army Ranger buddies. This is a small town. What happened on the freeway that day claimed the lives of six people from our town?"

"I understand how terrible it is to lose your dad. It must be doubly painful to lose your mom at the same time. Just ask them to keep it down."

"So that means they can stay?!"

I could hear the satisfaction booming through her voice and couldn't bear to say no. "Just ask them not to scream all the time," I said again.

"I will, sweetheart," she added.

I hung up the phone and went out the back door. Max had made it back to their yard, so I opened the gate and called him over. No one was there, so I grabbed my folding recliner, turned, and headed to the beach. They were all there, running along the shore. Even the baby was trying to walk stumbling along the way. I settled into my recliner and watched them from behind my sunglasses.

Emily looked to be around twenty-five, quite young to take on the responsibility of raising five kids. She was damn sexy with all those curves in the right places. I didn't usually pay much attention to shorter women, or should I say petite as they like to be called. This one had luscious curves, and that pink top she had on was stretched to the limit.

She must had forgotten her bra today those beautiful round orbs were standing at attention. I knew better than to get involved with someone like her; she practically had "stay away" tattooed on her forehead. I chuckled as the baby played in the water, and when she fell, I almost rushed to her rescue, but her brother beat me to it. I could hear her laughter from where I sat.

Yawning, I felt my eyelids growing heavy, and before I knew it, I had fallen asleep. When I woke up, someone had placed a child's Superman throw over me.

2

EMILY

MY FATHER AND HIS WIFE TRAGICALLY LOST THEIR LIVES IN A freak accident. A sandstorm caused a massive twenty-car pile-up on the freeway, and Dad and Maggie were trying to help people when they were struck by a truck and died at the scene. The devastation we felt was immeasurable.

My baby sister is too young to remember any of this, but she still looks around for her momma.

The first six months were incredibly challenging. It was particularly tough for my younger siblings to comprehend the loss of their parents. Some nights, all of us slept in my king-size bed. It became my responsibility to raise my brothers and baby sister. At the time, I held the position of head chef at a renowned restaurant.

When Jason called me and informed me about the tragedy, I didn't hesitate to rush to be with them. While achieving the position of top chef had been a lifelong dream since college graduation, my family too precedence over everything else. Witnessing their profound pain broke my heart.

Surprisingly, my father had no life insurance policies,

which was difficult to fathom considering his careful financial management. To settle their debts, I had to sell their home since I couldn't afford the monthly mortgage payments and cover all of their other debts. It was shocking to discover the extent of their financial obligations.

I vividly recall my father's philosophy on financial matters. He often said, "A person should never allow themselves to go into debt; it only hurts them and their loved ones." It appears he may have applied this principle selectively, mainly to my mother and me. His approached seemed to change significantly after marrying Maggie, who was considerably younger and more outgoing. He likely indulged her, which contributed to the financial situation they left behind.

Now that I'm the oldest in our family, we often discuss our future plans. I make sure my brothers are informed, and I rented a home for us on the beach. The rent for this place astoundingly affordable, and we were fortunate it was available. As I walked through the rooms, tidying up and straightening things, I pulled my long hair into a ponytail and headed to the kitchen to start preparing dinner.

Thinking about my mother still brought pain. I empathized with my siblings and their heartache. I was only thirteen when my mom succumbed to cancer. She was the one I was always closest to since my dad, an Army Ranger, was often away. After Mom's passing, Dad struggled to communicate with me since he never had time to learn sign language.

Back then, I didn't have hearing aids, so our conversations were limited. He took me with him wherever he was stationed until he retired, and we eventually settled in Maine, where he met Maggie. I was determined to do everything in my power to support my younger brothers and baby sister.

Taking on the responsibility of four active boys and a one-year-old baby girl was a challenge I had never encountered before. At thirty-one, I was considerably older than my siblings. Although I had seen them a few times a year, I wished I had spent more time with them.

Living far away and being engrossed in my career had prevented me from getting to know the kids as well as I should have. I hadn't even met baby Kelsey until this tragic event occurred. I had been too self-absorbed, focusing on my career goal of becoming the head chef at an upscale restaurant, a goal I had achieved. Looking back, I would give anything to change my priorities.

Upon my arrival at the neighbor's house where the boys were staying, they all rushed into my arms. We held each other in the middle of their neighbor's living room, shedding tears. After we had our emotional release, we got down to business and walked next door to their home. It was evident how difficult it was for them to step back inside with both their parents gone.

They appeared lost, not knowing where to turn. I watched as Mikey picked up his mom's sweater and took in her scent before breaking down in tears. I held him and sat with him on the sofa until his tears subsided. There was a lot of crying that first night and every night that followed for over a week. When the pastor brought Kelsey to us, I couldn't help but cry.

This beautiful baby girl was the apple of her parents' eye, and Maggie had shared countless pictures of Kelsey with me. I already loved her dearly. The pastor assisted me in making funeral arrangements, which depleted their savings. I was in a state of panic, wondering how I would manage. With what remained of my savings, I secured this house for us.

I had a candid discussion with the boys, sharing details about the available funds and our parents' outstanding debts. I didn't want them to think I had uprooted them from their home without a valid reason. We collectively decided to keep Maggie's van for transportation. My Cooper car, which I adored, had to be sold when we let go of their home.

Parting with my car was painful, but I understood that possessions were just that—material things. What truly mattered was my family. As we sorted through the rooms, packing items for sale and selecting keepsakes to retain, the process became emotionally exhausting. We donated the rest to a thrift store, which was a relief for all of us. The pastor informed us about this house, and we decided to make it our temporary home.

Our rental agent, Marge, arranged for some strong individuals to help us move our heavy belongings. She displayed remarkable kindness and understanding, offering support even when one of the kids would burst into tears. She embraced them and continued with the task at hand. I couldn't have managed without her.

In exchange for the affordable rent, Marge requested that we keep noise levels down when our neighbor was around. We were determined to establish a positive rapport with our new neighbor, or at least we hoped to. With my hands full, I had no time to dwell on the handsome man next door or anyone else. My days were filled with responsibilities.

I had just returned home after dropping the boys off at school when I saw Max leap over the fence. He made his way toward me as I held Kelsey. "Max, you're going to get us in trouble. It's only eight-thirty, and I'm sure your owner is still asleep, unaware that you've escaped again."

I opened the front door when I noticed my neighbor jogging down the beach. How I longed to run again. Running had always cleared the cobwebs from my head. I made a mental note that when I started earning more money, I would invest in one of those three-wheel baby strollers suitable for beach runs. I needed to exercise, as I felt my curves were becoming excessive. I watched as my neighbor ran up to us.

"Good morning, Emily."

"Good morning. I'm sorry, I don't know your name."

"It's Kash Walker."

"Hi, Kash. I hope you don't think I let your dog out. He jumped over the fence when he heard us. The kids were extra careful to be quiet. Getting ready for school this morning."

"I never thought you let him out."

"Oh, that's good to know. Well, goodbye," I said as I walked into the house leaving him standing there. Marge called me early this morning and told us the neighbor had asked if we could keep the noise down. So, there was no way in hell I was going to be friendly to my fink of a neighbor. Yet, I had to force myself not to look out the window to see where he went.

"I have some cooking to do, Kelsey baby. Do you want to sit in your highchair and watch me?" I said as I picked her up and secured her in her chair.

THE OWNER of the restaurant in Colorado offered to rent us a larger home for the kids, but they wanted to stay in their own school with their friends. So that's what we did. I started my own catering business. I could be at home with Kelsey during the day as I didn't think a daycare would be suitable for her.

In addition, chefs work long hours, and I didn't want to be away from the kids too much. I'd gotten a few orders for dinner parties, which was keeping us a float. All I had to do was cook the food. They had their own servers. Until the cash started coming in and I had the money to hire servers, this was my reality. I made Kelsey's breakfast and fed her. The morning was getting away from me. I still needed to plan those menus.

As I did every morning, I opened the blinds to let in the natural light. Through the window, I noticed a shadow passing by. A stunning blonde woman in a red convertible parked in front of the neighbor's house. When she stepped out of her car, her legs seemed as long as my entire body. I couldn't help but feel a pang of jealousy—okay, more than a little. I stopped growing in height when I was twelve, although not all of me stopped growing; some parts kept expanding if I don't watch what I eat. I used to wear heels to appear taller. But after cooking all day and into the evening, my feet and legs couldn't handle it, so I switched to flats.

I have to admit, I was nosey. I wanted to know what the neighbor and the blonde were doing. I watched as Kash answered the door. The woman threw her arms around him and their lips locked. Then they disappeared inside closing the door behind them. *Someone is going to get him some nooky this morning*—shame on me for thinking that. It's been a while since I've had anything.

Kelsey and I walked out back and enjoyed the peaceful view of the ocean. While I soaked in the tranquility, I began to make my meal plans for the three customers this week.

Suddenly Max, our neighbor's dog heard Kelsey in the back-yard and jumped over the fence.

Kelsey screamed with delight and clapped her hands. Max approached her with his tail flapping. She hugged his neck and planted a kiss on his furry head. I couldn't but laugh at their adorable interaction. She was so cute. "I'm going to wash your mouth before you kiss me again," Kelsey thought that was so funny that she started giggling.

I was almost finished with my meal plans when the gate to our back yard swung open, and Kash and blonde woman entered my back yard. *Does he get to walk into my backyard whenever he wants?*

"Max, you have to stop jumping the fence. I'm sorry, he jumps the wall every time he hears you in the yard."

Since I was facing him, I caught some of what he said. I was very good at reading lips. "Don't worry about it. Kelsey loves having him to play with." I decided right then to get a lock and put it on my gate.

"Didn't you hear us calling for Max?" the blonde woman asked.

Kash shot her an exasperated look, and I anticipated that he was about to explain that I couldn't hear unless I was facing her. However, I beat him to it. "No, I'm sorry, I didn't hear anything."

"No, I'm sorry I didn't hear anything."

"How could you not hear? You'd have to be deaf not to hear us."

"Janet, please," Kash growled. "I apologize for disturbing you. Let's go, Max."

I picked up Kelsey, preparing to head inside. Kash turned to leave but before he did I said, "If you don't mind Max being here, I don't mind. The children love playing with him."

"If you don't care, I guess he can. Either that or we build a higher fence."

I overheard the blonde woman mutter something, but I managed to read her lips. "How many kids does she have? Doesn't she know having large families is not the thing to do these days? She must have been fifteen when she started having kids." She even had the audacity to frown at me.

3

KASH

I hurriedly escorted Janet away from the gathering as soon as I could. I forgot how she acted like she was better than most people. But her envy towards Emily's alluring curves was unmistakable. Emily's magnetic, seductive voice only seemed to fuel Janet's jealousy further.

I was certain that my fling with Janet had reached its conclusion. How had I failed to notice her rudeness before? Perhaps it was because I was preoccupied with how quickly she shed her clothes a realization that now made me feel somewhat cheap. It wasn't like having sex with Janet was that memorable. Why did I keep dating her if we didn't have anything in common? It should be something you remember an hour later, after being with her.

My friend Luke was deeply in love with his wife, Missy, which made me question why I couldn't find something similar. But then I reminded myself that I had no desire for a committed relationship; my plate was already full with numerous ongoing projects. I didn't need more complications in my life right now.

When we got to the friend's house for dinner, I spotted

Emily and Jason carrying food containers through the back door. *She must be helping the caterer.* I wondered if she was going to serve the food. I walked inside with Janet and didn't have another thought about Emily.

I had seen some of my Ranger buddies, so I enjoyed the evening when we sat down to dinner. I realized how hungry I was. I looked around, but I didn't see Emily anywhere. The dinner was delicious. Melissa was getting all kinds of compliments on everything they ate.

"I'll tell Emily how much you enjoyed her meal."

"Are you talking about Emily Jones?" Catrina Richards asked. "I've been looking for her phone number. I lost my phone and half of my contacts. I heard about her family. It's truly heartbreaking."

"Yes, she moved back to Maine. She's only cooking now. She's starting a catering business so she can be at home with the children. If you want her for a dinner party, you need to call in advance. There is a waiting list, and you'll need to supply your own servers. Emily came home to care for her younger siblings. So, of course, they come first in her life. I'm glad she's home. I missed her when she moved away."

"I had no idea Emily was back. I'll definitely give her a call. I don't think I have her number either. Can I get her contact details before I leave? She has many friends in town, and her family's tragedy was truly devastating. She used to be the Top Chef at The Nest in Aspen, Colorado, right? I bet they hated to see her go," Sandy Sherman chimed in.

I LISTENED to the ladies talking about Emily. Then they started talking about their college days with her. So, she was a famous chef. She changed her life completely because she loves her younger siblings.

I felt Janet take my hand. I had to force myself not to pull it away. I noticed Janet talking about some of the other guests at least three times. And it wasn't nice gossip either. She never had anything nice to say about anyone and she was quickly getting on my nerves.

"Darling. I planned to spend the night at your place. Today was just the beginning of what I've been planning for us."

"I leave early in the morning for a meeting in Delaware, so I'll drop you off at your place when we leave here," I replied. I watched as she pouted, her bottom lip sticking out. I used to think that was adorable, and now it just turned me off. Tonight, I needed to have a frank conversation with her about ending our relationship, a task I hated doing. It was one of the reasons I hesitated to get involved in relationships with women; breakups could turn ugly.

"THANK YOU FOR YOUR HELP, Jason. I wouldn't have managed all these dishes without you."

"I'm glad I could help. Emily, your phone is ringing."

"Oh." Emily picked up her phone and looked at the screen. "Oh, it's my hearing aid doctor. Can you talk to him for me?" She handed the phone over to him. He was such a hard worker; he tried to do almost all of the heavy lifting, and he never complained about helping her.

"Yeah. Hello, this is Jason. I'm Emily's brother."

"Hi, Jason. Emily texted me and told me about what happened with her hearing aids. I have some excellent news for her. A customer ordered hearing aids just like Emily's, but he's changed his mind. He's already paid for them he doesn't want them anymore. Let Emily know she can come and pick them up if she wants. I'll wait at the office for her."

"I'll tell her right now. Thank you! We'll see you in a little bit."

"Emily, he has hearing aids for you. A customer ordered them and paid for them, but he no longer wants them. They're yours for free. The doctor said to come down and get them; he's waiting at his office until you get there," Jason said, excitedly.

"He has hearing aids for me? Oh, my lord, that's incredible. I'll get Kelsey. You get the boys. I'm going to be able to hear you guys. Those hearing aids cost four thousand dollars. I can't believe this is happening," I collected the kids from the teenager that was watching them for me.

We all piled into the van and drove to her doctor's office. The nurse warmly embraced Emily when we arrived. Emily had been seeing the same doctor since she lost her hearing at the age of ten.

"You kids can wait in the waiting room," the nurse suggested.

Emily shook her head. "No. I want to hear my family when I first put these hearing aids in. I lost mine when a stupid car tried to run me over on the sidewalk."

"I hope you reported it to the police."

"I did, but they never got back to me." Emily replied with a smile, the nurse shook her head in disbelief.

"Alright, everyone, follow me," she said looking at all the kids.

Emily was so excited, the tears welled up in her eyes as the doctor inserted the hearing aids.as the doctor put her hearing aids in her ears. Her brothers watched anxiously for her reaction, and then baby Kelsey looked at her and said, "Home." Tears streamed down Emily's face when she heard her brother's laughter "She wants to go home. It's her dinner time." The doctor wiped the tears off of his face with his large handkerchief. This was the most rewarding lie he had ever told. Emily's mother was a good woman who loved her daughter.

"How can I ever thank you? What if the man returns for his hearing aids?"

"He already went to Europe for his surgery."

"I didn't know you could have surgery for this. Does it work?"

"I'll have to wait and see what the man says about it. I'm just thrilled that you can hear your siblings no."

"Me too. Thank you."

"You're welcome. Drive carefully on the way home."

"I will. You do the same." The doctor patted her on the back and walked her to the front door.

Emily laughed all the way home. Her brothers wouldn't stop talking, and Kelsey wouldn't stop saying, "Eat." She realized she was starting to feel happy again. *I don't think I've been really happy since my mom died.* "Look at the moon. It's so big tonight. Let's go on the beach after dinner tonight."

"Yeah, that'll be lots of fun," Tommy agreed, wearing a broad smile.

4

KASH

I HAD A POUNDING HEADACHE, AND DESPERATELY NEEDED some sleep. Damn, who would have thought that breaking up with Janet would be so draining? She refused to accept our breakup, insisting that it wasn't happening.. She swore we were not breaking up.

The woman had the nerve to tell me it was because I loved her, and it scared the hell out of me. I hope tonight is the last scene I have with her. It's been over a week since we broke up. I am in dire need of some Advil.

You could have knocked me over when she walked into my house uninvited. I needed a shower and a bed. I looked at the clock and saw it was eight p.m., the perfect time for bed.

When I opened my eyes, the sun was shining through the shutters. My phone started ringing. In my groggy state, I almost knocked my gun off the nightstand. I grabbed my phone. I was ready to tear into whoever was calling me this early. "Hello,"

"Hey, buddy. We leave in an hour. Where are you?" a voice on the other end urgently inquired.

"What time is it?" I asked.

"It's noon."

"What! Damn, I'm on my way." I can't believe I slept that long. I hastily grabbed my gun, then my bag, before heading out the door. Fuck, what am I going to do with Max? Dare I ask my neighbor for a favor, even though she didn't seem to like me much? To hell with it. I ran over and knocked on the door. Myself momentarily stunned by her appearance. She was dressed in a long colorful skirt and a peasant-style blouse. Her long hair cascading down her back. She looked like she stepped right out right out of the sixties. "You look beautiful!" Regretting my choice of words. *Why the f*** did I say that?*

"Why, thank you! How can I help you?" she replied.

"I know I have no right to ask, but I overslept, and I'm going out of the country. Can I please leave Max here with you? I forgot to call the kennel. I could take him to my mom's if you'd rather not watch him."

"Of course you can. Don't worry about Max. He enjoys being here."

"I'll go get him."

"That's okay. Max is already here."

"He is?" I was surprised, and she chuckled.

"Thank you." I said, turning to leave. Under my breath, I couldn't help but mutter, "Why does she hate me?"

"I don't hate you. I just don't like you. But I would never hate anyone. Isn't that a sin?" she replied.

"You can hear me?"

"Yes, my doctor had these spare hearing aids that a man ordered, but later went to Europe for surgery and no longer needs them. My doctor gave them to me. I'm eternally grateful to him. I can hear my family now, and I'll know if they are noisy so they won't bother you."

Did I just see her wipe a tear? "I'm genuinely happy for you. I really am. The kids haven't been noisy. I'm sorry for that first day; I was exhausted."

"Thank you for saying that. Well, you better get going. We'll take good care of Max. Thanks for letting him stay here with the kids."

"He's practically here all the time anyway," I remarked before walking away.

Emily chuckled as she shut the door and returned to her kitchen to finish cooking. Then she stopped and grabbed a pan of hors d'oeuvres. She threw them into a paper bag and ran them out to Kash as he backed out of his driveway. "Kash, take these. I made way too many."

"Really. Thanks. I'm starving."

"Don't mention it," she replied with a smile before heading back inside.

THAT WAS A SURPRISE. I reached into the bag and pulled out one of the hot meatballs Emily had made. They were delicious, and my tastebuds thanked me. He had devoured almost half of them before he got to the airport.

Ryan Grant glanced at me and said, "It's about damn time. We're going to stop and pick up Angel. One of the people we're rescuing is injured. Angel offered to come along. But he said don't think this is going to be an everyday thing. What are you eating?"

"Hors d'oeuvres."

"Where the hell did you get them?" Ryan asked as he stuck his hand in the bag and got a couple of them. "Damn, these are good. Who made them?"

"My neighbor. She's a chef."

"So, you and your chef neighbor got something going on?"

"No, she doesn't like me. She loves Max though. He's at her house more than he's at mine. She's raising her five younger siblings."

Ryan nodded. "Emily Jones, right? Your neighbor is Emily."

"Yeah, do you know her?"

"I went to college with her. We were her guinea pigs when she was testing her delicious meals."

He took another bite of the meatball and added, "I heard about the accident. I'll visit Emily when I get back. She's a wonderful person."

"She seems younger than you. I thought she was around twenty-five," Kash interjected, sticking his hand in the bag and pulling out two of the meatballs."

What are you eating?" Matt asked, sitting down next to us.

"Snacks," I replied.

"They're great. Why have you eaten all of them?" Matt asked.

"Because they are mine."

"Did your girlfriend make them?" He said.

"No, I don't have a girlfriend. My neighbor made them."

"What happened to the long-legged blonde?" Matt asked.

"She didn't have a good personality. I don't want to be with someone with a mean heart."

"Who cares about her personality? What happened to you? To hell with her character, she was hot, hot, hot!"

"I'll tell you what, Matt, you can have her." I retorted, watching the disgusted look on his face.

"I don't want anything already used by one of my friends."

I RECALLED the story about Matt and his fiancée. For some reason, Lara broke up with him. She never did say why. It damn near broke Matts's heart into a million pieces.

Looking at Matt. "Do you know Emily Jones?"

"Yeah, I went to school with her. I think she lives in Colorado now."

"She did until her father and his wife died. Now Emily has moved back to caring for her five younger siblings."

"Oh wow, that was her dad. I heard about that accident. That's too bad. I feel bad for the family. Didn't her dad marry and have a bunch of kids? Did she make the snack?"

"Yeah, didn't you hear me? She's my neighbor, and she has the children."

"I thought you didn't allow kids to live next door."

"My mom rented it to Emily. What am I supposed to do? She has all those kids."

"Is she still a hot little thing?"

I didn't like the way Matt posed that question. "Yes. It's killing me. She doesn't do anything to try and show how sexy she is. She's always carrying Kelsey around. One day, I went over there to find Max sleeping with the baby in her crib. Emily had to take the side of her crib down so Max could sleep with the baby. My dog doesn't want to come home. He loves those kids."

"Why don't you buy them their own German Shepherd."

"Then they would have two of them." I opened the file and went through it to change the subject. "So, we're going back to Afghanistan. How many people are we getting out of there? Whose plane are we taking?"

"We have Mark's plane. It's pretty big, so we should be able to get a bunch of them out of there."

"Okay, let's get down to business," I said, bringing out the maps.

"We'll have to be in and out of there quick. I don't want to see any of those tanks we gave the Taliban coming at us. The people we are going in there to rescue are Americans who have family over here. And the family members here want their family back. They said they couldn't get the government to listen to them."

"That has been happening a lot, unfortunately. There will be others who will try getting into the plane. If they are women and children, we'll take them. Where are we picking up Angel?"

Matt shook his head. "He'll meet us at the first stop. I hope he's sober. I can't handle a drunk Angel. He's an immense pain in the neck. We got into a damn fistfight the last time I was around him while he was drinking."

I looked over at Matt, ready to make things clear. "He doesn't drink like that anymore. He got whatever out of his system that caused him to be self-destructive," Matt said.

"Good, I didn't like seeing him like that. Does he plan on going back to work?"

"I don't know. We'll have to wait and see."

5

EMILY

I WAS SO EXHAUSTED AND READY FOR BED. I HADN'T STOPPED since I crawled out of bed at five this morning. I had a large order to fulfill, so I cooked non-stop. I couldn't help but think about the need for a bigger stove. I required at least eight burners and three ovens to meet the increasing demand for my dishes.

Christmas was approaching rapidly, and the influx of orders had already begun. I made a mental note to go online and search for a reasonably priced restaurant stove. I knew Jason could assist me with this; he was quite the expert when it came to finding deals on Craig's List. Within moments, my heavy eyelids closed, and I drifted into a deep sleep.

I overslept. I had to feed the boys cereal for breakfast. They loved it. I gave Brian three cupcakes for his principal. "Tell her I said hello."

"Will she know you are bribing her?"

Emily laughed. "Probably. I love you kids. I'll see you when you get out of school."

"I'll start looking for a stove for you," Jason said, hugging me.

"Thank you, Jason."

I cheated and drove by Starbucks. Even though I promised myself I would never again spend that much money on a cup of coffee, I treated myself to a Caramel Frappe. I had a lot to do today. My phone went off. It was Jason. "Hello, Jason. Is everything okay?"

"My principal wants to talk to you. Can you come to my school?"

"I'll be right there. Is something wrong?" I asked.

"No, I have to go to my class."

"I'll see you later today." *Why does the principal want to see me?* My stomach started burning. I felt like I was in school again, and the principal called me to the office. I've never even met anyone in Jason's school. I'll have to make sure I become more involved with his school projects. I pulled into the parking lot, walked around, and took Kelsey out of the back seat. I felt like I was thirteen again, walking into the office.

"Hello, I'm Emily Jones. The principal wants to see me."

"Emily."

I turned around and was surprised to find one of my childhood best friends standing there—a friend from before my mom got cancer and died. I was so excited to see her standing there. I screamed and ran to embrace her. We hugged each other. It brought me back to when my mom was living, seeing my friend again.

"Cricket, are you the principal?" I asked.

"Yes, come into my office. I only just now found out you were Jason's sister. I've thought about you so often. Someone told me you lived in Colorado. That you were a head chef at a fancy restaurant."

"I was living there. But I live here with the kids now. They come first in my life."

"I swear, Emily, you are the best sister. Just look at you. I swear you haven't grown an inch since eighth grade. Well, some of you have grown," Cricket chuckled.

I laughed, knowing just what she meant. "Yeah, I'm short and chunky."

"You are not chunky, Emily. Look at me. I still have my baby fat. You are doing an amazing job, and few sisters would give up everything and take on what you have. I'm proud of you, and know your mom would be too."

"Thank you. How are your parents?"

Cricket's face soured. "My parents sold their house and moved to Honduras. They have a beachfront property there. I see them once a year, and that's when I visit them. You'd think they didn't have a daughter. Whenever I call them, they're always busy. I doubt I'll visit them anymore."

"I'm sorry to hear that. I hardly saw my dad after he married Maggie. I never met Kelsey, this little sweetheart, until I came back to take care of them. My biggest regret is that I lived so far away from the kids. I'm going to adopt them as soon as I can. I don't want any of Maggie's family trying to take them away from me."

"Do you think they would try to do that?"

"They were around for a while until they realized there was no money, then they left. Jason said our dad didn't want them coming around because they were strange."

"Your dad didn't have any life insurance. That doesn't sound like him," Cricket whispered.

"I know, I was surprised too. We had to sell their home," I whispered, ensuring our conversation remained private. "They had so much debt. We had to sell everything to pay it off."

"You are doing an amazing job."

"Thank you. I'm doing it because I love them more than anything. I better get going. I have so much cooking to do. Wait, are you married?"

"No, I was, but it didn't work out."

"I'm sorry to hear that."

"Me too. There was another reason I brought you here. Jason asked me what we were going to do with that huge stove outback. We were planning to have the Humanity store pick it up. But if you want it, it's yours."

"What? Does it work?"

"Yes, the school board bought us a new one. Let's look at it. I think it's only a few years old. I was surprised when the new stove arrived. I don't know who ordered it. So now you can have this one."

I couldn't believe my luck; the stove was way more than I could have ever imagined. "Yes, I want this stove. Thank you so much. I have a catering business. I cook the food, and clients hire their own servers. It takes me forever to cook three different menus."

"I know you'll do great. You have always been a go-getter."

"Have I? I can't remember that about myself," I said, smiling.

"You've got to be kidding. Everything you do, you tackle with full force. Remember when you wanted to be a singer? You had your mom buy you a guitar, and you learned how to play a song, and you sang at the talent contest. All the kids went wild. They loved it."

"Yeah, it was pretty bad," I chuckled.

Cricket joined in the laughter. "Yeah, but the kids all loved it anyway."

"I'm glad you're here. I'll see if I can find someone to get this stove out of here today. You should come to dinner on Wednesday. I only prepare dinner for others three days a week. I enjoy spending all my time with the kids." I wrote my address down for her.

"Wow, that's a nice area to live in."

"Yeah, we lucked out because the kids' pastor told me about it. And the woman who rented it, her husband, was in the Army Rangers with my dad, so we got a great price."

"What happened with your hearing? You seem to be able to hear well now."

"Yeah, they came out with these new hearing aids that work great with my hearing loss." I chose not to tell her about my free hearing aids; no need for her to think I was in dire straits.

Cricket gave me a warm hug; she was genuinely happy for me. "Wow, that's wonderful. I still remember how to sign. We have a student here with hearing impairment, and I've seen Jason signing with him."

"I feel sorry for anyone with a hearing problem. Maybe he can get himself some hearing aids if he has any slight hearing at all."

"His family could never afford to buy hearing aids for him."

"I wonder if he ever had any hearing when he was younger."

"Hmm, I don't know."

Later that day, I managed to arrange for a large truck to help us move the stove, from some old friends who had helped us with our move. Then, I called Bella to see if her brothers could assist me with moving the stove. She graciously volunteered their services, and we shared a laugh over it. With three guys lined up, I thought it might be enough to tackle the hefty stove, but I knew I needed at least two more. Just as I was contemplating this, my phone rang again, and I answered.

"Hey, Emily, I hear you need help with moving a stove."

"Who is this?"

"Sorry, this is Ryes Cohen. I'm married to Riley, Isabella's sister. Since I'm here, I'll go with Owen and the others. We'll stop and pick up my buddy Ash Beckham. We'll see you at four at the school."

"Thank you. Yes, I'll meet you there. The truck will be there. The driver can't pick anything up. He hurt his back."

"We'll make sure he doesn't lift a finger," Rye's said before hanging up.

"Thank you!" I was so excited. I was getting my stove. *Now, where am I going to put it? I'll have to move the stove in the kitchen.* "Oh lord, Kelsey, what will we do with this stove? Let me put you in your walker, and you can play with Max while I measure this spot. Keep your fingers crossed that it fits."

6

KASH

DAMN, THIS IS SO MUCH WORSE THAN WE PLANNED. NICHOLAS assured us everyone would be ready to go, but Angel and the rest of us were furious. When we arrived at our designated spot, we found that our contact had been shot, and Angel worked tirelessly to save him while the others remained in hiding.

"We can't leave!" the man exclaimed.

I fixed my gaze on him. "Where are the people we are supposed to pick up and fly out of here?"

"They are hiding. Those innocent people are terrified for their lives. The Taliban is abducting girls and handing them over to men. Please don't leave them here."

I nodded, realizing I knew I couldn't leave anyone behind. "Tell me where they are. I won't leave them behind."

Angel slammed his fist on the table. "Damn it, Kash. You're going to get yourself killed. I don't think you should do this."

"Ryan, what do you say?"

"I'm in. Tell us where they're hiding and how many we need to rescue."

Nicholas looked at his buddy. "I'm not sure about the exact number. They're hiding in the back of their church, which is about five miles from here. Once you reach the people, the women have the vehicles ready. You just need to get them here as fast as possible," Nicholas said.

"We'll have the plane ready at the end of the runway, so you won't need to cover that distance. Matt, are you getting this? You'll have to circle and taxi to the end of the runway," Nicholas said, "or do I need to repeat everything?

"I've got it."

I looked at Nicholas. "You realize you can't stay here anymore; they know you were an Army Ranger, and your cover has been blown."

"I'm aware."

"Let's move." I turned to Ryan Grant. "Grab as much ammo as you can carry."

We set off at a sprint. Ryan took the jeep's front seat, and we raced towards the church, fully aware of the danger. My eyes stung from the blowing sand, but I dared not blink. Ryan and I understood the gravity of the situation. We parked the jeep behind the church, and I knocked on the door. An American woman opened it, confirming we'd arrived at the right place, but I noticed a lack of other vehicles.

"Where are the other vehicles?"

"We only have one left; the other was riddled with bullet holes."

I looked at Ryan; he shrugged. "Can anyone else drive?"

"I can," a seventy-five-year-old woman said, and then a very pregnant woman stepped forward. "I can drive," she said.

"Let's get going." We loaded up the available vehicles,

but there were still too many people who had to run. "Ryan and I will stay behind with those on foot." I glanced around and saw some small children. I picked them up and placed them on the laps of the older women in the vehicles.

We hadn't gone far when I spotted dust in the distance. "Hurry, they're approaching." I saw Angel get in one of the vehicles near the plane, and the pregnant woman got in the other one. We loaded the kids into the vehicles, and they sped off. Only a few remained running. I stayed behind them, knowing I had to stop these pursuers, but I couldn't identify them. I witnessed the plane getting loaded, and I felt a wave of relief.

When I reached the ladder, I jumped up and felt the bullet hit my leg. I fell, and Ryan picked me up and threw me over his shoulder and climbed the ladder where we were pulled inside the door. The plane was already going down the runway. We pulled the door shut and I leaned against the wall.

"What the hell happened?" Angel demanded.

"I hurt my leg."

"You didn't fucking hurt your leg. You've been shot. Lay down." Angel looked at me and added, "This is going to hurt you more than it does me. I have to take this bullet out."

"I know. Just do it." That's when I heard the pregnant lady cry out. "Check on her first."

I kept my eyes closed and tried not to listen to the woman delivering the baby. But she was too loud. Angel came back and got his bag.

"The baby is in the wrong position, and I have to turn it, or both of them will die. Are you going to be okay until I've finished?"

"Yes, go. I'll be fine." I laid there trying to drown out the sounds of the poor woman's cries as Angel tried to turn her baby. I started singing an old country song out loud so the kids wouldn't be frightened. My thoughts wondered to my neighbor. It's been three weeks since I'd been home. I wonder if my dog missed me or if they turned Max against me. I heard a scream and then the cry of a newborn baby.

Thirty minutes later, Angel was probing my leg. I had to suppress the urge to cry out. "Do you have anything for pain?"

"I'll give us both a shot of whiskey in a minute. There it is. Here, bite down on this," Dr. Angel Davis said as he threw a piece of wood at me.

"Where the hell did you get this?"

"On my beach. For some reason, I knew I would need it."

I passed out. When I woke up, we were flying over the ocean. "How long have I been out?" I asked Angel, who was tying a white piece of cloth around my leg.

"About an hour. You're all set."

"I don't remember getting that whiskey."

Angel laughed as he poured me a shot of whiskey in an old tin coffee cup. I swallowed it and coughed. "What the hell was that?"

"That's my homemade whiskey."

"It's like poison."

"I poured it on your leg; it has enough alcohol in it to kill all the germs that can crawl into your wound."

"It's still burning my stomach."

Angel chuckled. "It'll help you sleep."

"How are the mom and baby doing?"

"They're doing good. She is so happy to be getting out of this country."

"I think we did well this time around," I said.

"You know, Kash, you can't keep this up. The Taliban

will eventually shut down all the airports, and there won't be nowhere to land," Angel said.

"I know, but as long as they're Americans in Afghanistan, I will do everything I can to help get them out."

7

EMILY

I chuckled as Owen Sanger shared the story of attempting to move that massive stove into the truck.

"I went there thinking, Wow, I remember that beauty, Emily Jones. I'll move that stove, and then I'll ask her out. I bent down to pick up that stove and heard a ripping sound. My pants completely ripped from the crotch all the way up the back. My favorite shorts."

I couldn't help but laugh. "You had definitely worn them out. I thought we would all bust a gut listening to that sound. It felt so good to laugh like that."

"Hey, you're feeding us. The way I see it, we are the winners here. Thanks for the invitation," Owen replied.

"You're welcome. With this stove, my catering business will be so much easier. Thank you, everyone, for all your help." We were sitting in the backyard of our house, dinner was over, and people started going home. I noticed a vehicle pull into the driveway next door. I watched Kash get out with a pair of crutches. Standing up, I walked over there. Sometimes, like now, I wished I wasn't one of those people who just walked into the middle of trouble.

Kash wasn't at all happy to see me. "Are you throwing a party?"

"No, it was just dinner for my friends."

"Hey, Kash, what happened?" Owen and Ash walked up and stood behind me.

"My leg got in the way of a bullet. If you will excuse me, I need sleep." He looked at me. "I hope you won't be having parties over there too often."

"I won't dignify that with a response," I said. "Have you eaten?"

"NOT YET," another guy said, coming around the back of the truck carrying two duffel bags.

"Please help yourself. I made a buffet-style dinner for us tonight."

"I'm Angel. Are you the one who made those meatballs? They were delicious." Angel handed the bags to Owen as he followed me toward the food.

"Thank you. Are you staying at Kash's tonight? If I prepare a platter for you to take over there, will you not tell him I sent it. I'm afraid he would feed it to Max."

Angel chuckled. "So you are the one his dog loves?"

"No, it's her. Follow me, and I will show you." I led him where Max slept next to Kelsey in the bed.

He held his out hand. "I didn't get your name, I'm Angel Davis." This time he told me his full name.

"Emily Jones."

"It's nice meeting you, Emily."

"You too, Angel. Let's grab that food." I retrieved a large tin pan and began filling it up with food. "I don't know why I want to feed him. He's rude and never has anything nice to say to me. I thought he was being kind by letting Max stay here. But no, he couldn't wait to complain about my dinner party. We are so quiet; we don't make any noise. We're afraid he'll call my rental lady, Marge, and tell her we are noisy. He's already done it once."

"He's always been a little grumpy. Plus, he drank my homemade whiskey. I'm sure that didn't help."

"That could be true."

"But hey, it's something we have all said about Kash. He doesn't like change of any kind, and his mom rented the house to you. He doesn't like to be around kids. He thinks they are noisy."

"What? Are you telling me Marge is Kash's mom? I might have told her he was a snitch because he called her to complain about the kids."

"Don't worry about it. Kash is mostly all talk. He's actually a nice guy. I have to get this food over to Kash's place. I'll be around for a few days. I want to keep an eye on Kash's leg."

"Are you a doctor?"

"Yes, I am. I'm not practicing right now. I better get this food over to Kash."

"I hope his leg is going to be alright."

"He'll be fine. Don't worry about Kash. He's survived bullet wounds before."

"I can't believe she had a large dinner party," Kash remarked as he devoured the food. "Where did you get this sweet tea? It's so refreshing. This food is delicious."

"Where do you think I got it? I've been next door and only next door. She did some bartering; the guys moved a restaurant stove over to her house, and she cooked them dinner."

"She put a giant stove in there. I wonder what she did with the stove that was already there. I'm sure it's in the rental agreement that she can't swap it out. If she's starting a catering business because she needs money, then why is she renting my house next door? It rents for four thousand a month."

"Why are you being so hard on Emily? I'm sure she's done nothing wrong. Ask your mom how much her rent is. Is it because you want her, and that pisses you off?"

Kash grabbed his phone. "Hi Mom, I'm home."

"It's about time. Why do you have to keep this up? You're all I have. Every time you take one of those trips, it almost kills me." Kash held the phone away from his ear.

"Why do you ask the same question when I return from a job?" Kash asked.

"I have to ask you the same question every time you come back home from being overseas, so it will sink in your head how dangerous it is." his mom lectured him.

"I'm sorry, Mom. I won't be taking as many trips." He wasn't about to mention the bullet in his leg. "Mom, how much do you rent my house next door for?"

"Why are you asking now? You never even look in the bank account in which I deposit the money."

"Mom, it's still my house, and I like to keep track of the income."

"Well, I've been renting it for four thousand, you know that."

"That's what I thought. Is that what Emily is paying?"

"Emily, well, Emily can't afford to pay that kind of rent."

"How much is she paying?"

"She's paying eight hundred."

"What? She's only paying eight hundred dollars. Why would you rent my house to her for eight hundred dollars?"

"Because she can't afford to pay any more than that. You're wealthy. Why does it bother you so much? When she can afford more, she'll buy her own house."

"Because she can afford to throw a big dinner party and feed a dozen people, she must have some money."

"You're an ass. Owen bought all of that food. I was invited as well. I assure you she doesn't have hidden money. I'm not going to kick her out. If you want to, then you do it. Otherwise, stop complaining like an old man all the time," Marge demanded.

He looked at the phone. "My mom hung up on me."

"I don't blame her; I would do the same thing. I'm going to bed. Damn, you are worse than an old man."

"I can hear you," I said.

"I hope so. I said it loud enough," Angel said, laughing.

I limped into the bathroom and took a shower. As I got out, I remembered I hadn't put the leftover food away. "This will make a perfect lunch," I thought as I put the food away. I stepped outside to see if my dog had returned home.

I heard Emily softly singing while she cleaned up. Doesn't she know how good a deal she's getting on the house? It's a four-bedroom, four-bathroom. It's not even about the money. Hell, I am a grumpy old man. What the hell is wrong with me? Why does it bother me so much that she lives next door with those kids? I'll change my attitude, I promised myself.

I reached for the phone and called my mom back. "Sorry, Mom. I swear I'll be a better person."

"You are a wonderful person with a big heart. What happened is that you and Emily got off on the wrong foot the first time you met. Emily is like a mother hen with those kids. I'm sorry I rented your house so cheaply. I'll explain everything to Emily, and she can start looking for another place to live. I got carried away when the pastor told me about Emily and those kids."

"No, you're right. I have more money than I know what to do with. I don't mind Emily and the kids living there. Anyway, I'm sorry. I promise to be nice to Emily. Besides, she's been feeding me."

"Okay, sweetheart, thank you. I'll see you in a day or two."

"Goodbye, Mom." Sometimes, I disgusted myself. I'll be nice to Emily and the kids. With that decision made, I went to bed.

8

KASH

"WHY IS SHE SCREAMING?" I DEMANDED TO KNOW FROM Angel.

"Don't ask me. Why is your dog howling?"

"Am I going to have to go over there? My God, what could be wrong with her? You're a doctor. Go see if there is anything wrong with that baby."

There was a banging on the door. When I opened it, Emily and a crying Kelsey stood there. Emily had tears in her eyes.

"I don't know what to do?" she cried.

"Mac!" Kelsey screamed at the top of her lungs.

She wants Max. "Can she say hello to him, please?"

"He's only been home for two hours."

"She hasn't stopped crying for two hours. I have a dinner party tonight and have to cook for ten people."

"Maybe this will make Max stop howling," I said, wanting to pull her into my arms so she would stop crying. "Max, get in here. Kelsey has completely ruined my dog," I said. I was ferocious. "He scared other people. Now, if he's here, all he does is cry to be back at your house." I watched as Emily put Kelsey down, and the German Shepherd smiled as Kelsey ran to him on her chubby little legs and wrapped her arms around him. Her face was beet red from crying. Tears ran down her face, and she wouldn't let go of my dog. Max kissed her face all over it, and she kissed him back.

"What are we going to do about this?" I asked, looking at Emily.

"Maybe if Max could visit for a couple of hours a day," she said, wiping her eyes, "I think maybe Kelsey won't scream. I don't know how to get her to stop crying once she starts."

"Have you spoiled her?" I asked.

"I don't think so. I'm sure I don't do any more than Maggie did," Emily said looking confused.

"You carry her everywhere," I said.

"I get from one spot to another faster that way," she explained.

"I know, but I think when some of my friends' kids were her age, they just walked slowly next to them."

"Really? I'm not sure I can do that. It'll take some prac-tice. I'm used to moving fast," she sniffed.

I looked at her. *Is she crying again?* "I'm sure you are doing a great job." I watched her shake her head.

"There is so much to do. I don't know if I'm doing it right or not. My mother raised me. When she died, there was only me. My dad was there but wasn't really there if you know what I mean. I had my friends when we moved back here, but I wasn't around any babies."

Her tears were falling faster than any storm I'd ever been in. I looked at Angel. He got up and got Emily some tissues.

I didn't even know what to say. "I could never do what you're doing. Raising five kids. You should get a trophy for what you've taken on."

I SHOOK MY HEAD. What is wrong with me? Why am I crying at my enemy's house? I ran my fingers through my hair, but it was so tangled I had to pull my fingers out. I had to think for a moment. I don't believe I combed my hair today. The tears started falling again. "Oh brother, I am so sorry. Wow, I don't know what came over me." I took a deep breath. "Okay, I'm all better. Thank you for listening to me. Good-bye." I got up quickly and walked outside. I was back on my doorstep when it dawned on me. I had forgotten Kelsey. *How can I go back over there?*

"EMILY." I slowly looked up, and Angel was carrying Kelsey while Max followed behind. "We weren't sure if you wanted Kelsey and Max to stay at Kash's house for two hours or for him to be over here."

I took a deep breath. "I am so sorry. I always have a bad day on this date. I found my mom in her bed, dead on this day. And even though it's been years, I still miss her so much," I whispered while more tears fell.

Angel nodded his head slowly. "I'm sorry. I know how you feel. My day is August tenth. I found my sister in her bedroom. She had hung herself. Don't tell a soul I told you this. No one needs to know our business."

I could have kissed him. He was so sexy and thoughtful. But he wasn't the one my body wanted. "Thank you for understanding. I promise my crying is over. Now, I need to get busy with my menu. I have two dinners to deliver tonight."

"I'll see you around."

I watched Angel walk back to Kash's house. I knew he wouldn't mention my mom. "Okay, the first thing we will do on my next day off is to get you a dog from the dog shelter." Kelsey didn't even hear me. She was busy with Max. "Two hours, Kelsey. After that, Max goes home."

The time got away from me. Before I knew it, the boys were home. Kelsey was sleeping with Max on the floor. I picked her up to carry her to bed and asked Jason to take Max back to Kash. I fixed them a snack and finished cooking. I was so happy to have gotten the stove, so I had plenty of room to do all of my cooking. I put Kelsey in the high chair and called the boys inside to eat.

We sat at the table for dinner. I promised myself we would always do that for every meal. I remember my mom telling me always have your meal at the table. That's where you learn how everyone's day went. I smiled at all of the kids as they started eating their dinner. "How was everyone's day?"

"I saw Mary Sue hit Johnny today," Tommy said, wiping his face off with his napkin.

"Why did she hit him?"

"Because he called her fatty."

"That wasn't nice. If Johnny is that mean, I don't want you playing with him."

"Okay. I wouldn't ever be mean."

"I know that, sweetie. Jason, how was your day?"

"Do you remember the boy who can't hear? Some of the boys made fun of him. So, I kind of got into a fight. My principal is going to call you. I'm sorry. But I had to do something."

"OF COURSE YOU DID. Before my mom was able to get my hearing aids, a few kids made fun of me. Cricket stuck up for me. Not that she needed to. I could stick up for myself. Over time, those kids apologized. But the damage was already done. Every time I looked at those kids, I remembered what they said to me. I'm sure Cricket remembered that as well. "Never hurt someone on purpose." I looked around at my boys and made eye contact. "Think to yourself, will it hurt that person's feelings if I say this? If you think the answer is yes, don't say it."

I WAS JUST ABOUT to knock on Emily's back door when I heard her talking. The door was open, but the screen door was shut. What she said hit me in the gut. I wondered who had made fun of her when she was a little girl who couldn't hear anything. She would have had to sit up front close to the teacher to see their lips moving. I felt like I could kick their ass if I knew who it was. I wondered why I felt that way.

I TURNED AROUND and hobbled to my house. I left the gate open in case Max wanted to visit with Kelsey. I looked at Angel. "Do you want to order pizza?"

"No, I ordered dinner for us from Emily. It'll be here at six."

"How did you do that?"

"She has a catering business. I had two different meals to choose from. I ordered us the chicken. It'll be here any time now."

"I didn't realize you could order meals."

"I don't know if she actually does this for just anyone. But I set up an entire week of dinners. Since I'll be here for the week, I wanted to make sure I have food to eat. Now, neither of us has to cook dinner."

"I THINK you wanted to make sure she makes money. I guess I could ask Mom to throw a large dinner party. I suppose we know other people who can have dinner parties. When are you moving back here? That big beach house is going to rot away. Every time I walk down the beach, I check it to ensure no one has broken into it."

"I have my cleaning lady go there every Friday to clean it?"

"Why? You are never there."

"Because she counts on that income. She doesn't have her husband's income anymore. He died a few years ago. She needs that little check to help her with groceries or bills."

"Every time I see you, I learn something new about you. Why did you turn to the bottle?"

"What do you mean?"

"You turned into a drunk. That's what I'm talking about."

"I did not. I was making whiskey. How else would I have found out whether my whiskey is good? There was no one else to try it out on."

"Is that true?"

"Hell, yes, it's true. Even though I did stop having headaches and drinking early in the morning because I had to keep testing."

I laughed. "You're an ass." The doorbell went off, and Angel got up to get it as I went in and set the table.

9

KASH

I knocked on Emily's door. Angel was returning to his island the next day, and I wanted to give Emily her dishes and tell her how much we enjoyed the dinners; after knocking on her door and ringing the doorbell a few times, she still didn't answer. Then I heard Max barking inside the house. An uneasy feeling washed over me, and I followed my instincts, turning the doorknob and entering her home. I couldn't see anyone but thought I had heard Emily talking to the baby.

"Emily, can you hear me?" I called out as I was further into the house. I checked the rooms and set the dishes on the kitchen counter. I spotted Max standing in the doorway. I walked to where he was and saw Emily wrapping Kelsey in a blanket. "Emily, what's wrong with Kelsey?" I realized she couldn't hear me. She didn't have her hearing aids in. I didn't want to scare her, so I picked up a toy and tossed it in the corner. She glanced at it and then turned to me.

"Thank God you are here. The baby is sick. I was going to take her to your house so Angel could check her? Is he still there?"

Her face was deathly white. "Yes, here, let me carry her. Follow me. Do you have a baby thermometer?"

"Yes," Emily replied, getting the thermometer.

I watched as she took in a deep breath and held it before letting it out slowly. Emily grabbed some things she thought we would need. She followed me as I carried the baby to my house. I could hear her talking to herself the entire walk over there.

"She is my baby. I love her so much, I'm scared."

I tapped her on the shoulder. "It's going to be okay. Babies get sick."

I could tell Emily didn't realize she spoke out loud.

"I'm sorry for saying my thoughts out loud. Kelsey is my baby, and I'm responsible for everything now."

We entered my house and saw Angel walking down the hallway with a towel around his waist.

"Angel, can you check Kelsey? Emily is scared that she might be sick."

"Let me get some clothes on." He walked into his room and came out a minute later wearing basketball shorts.

"Let me see her. Emily, stop worrying about Kelsey. Babies get fevers." Emily didn't say anything.

"She doesn't have her hearing aids in. She has to see you talking."

Angel tapped Emily on the shoulder. "Where are your hearing aids?"

"I gave them to a high school student. He could hear slightly if the person talking to him was facing him. Now he can hear all the time." She wiped a tear from her cheek.

Angel looked at me and shook his head. He carried Kelsey to the sofa and sat down. Max was right next to him. He tapped Emily on the shoulder. "Why do you think

Kelsey is sick? Look at her. She's laughing at Max. She's a little warm, but babies get warm."

"She has a fever. She didn't want her breakfast. I had her sleep with me last night, so I would know if she woke up because of me not having my hearing aids." She looked over at Kash. "Max slept in my bed. So, you have to watch Kelsey while I shower."

Angel shook his head. "She has an average temperature for a child. She looks to be cutting a tooth in the back. She's very healthy."

"So, I don't have to take her to the emergency room."

"No, you don't. Now tell me, why the hell would you give your hearing aids away?"

"I told you the boy hasn't been able to hear in years. Some bullies made fun of him at school. Don't you think it's more important if a child in school can hear? I couldn't wear those hearing aids, knowing he couldn't hear. So, Jason told him they were extras. Jason says he's always smiling now.

"I can save up and get me another pair later." I watched her wipe her tears with her shirt sleeve. "I'll call my ENT and tell him to order me another pair. Thank you again. I don't know why I'm always scared something will happen to Kelsey."

I looked at her; I needed to understand. "How do you answer your phone?"

"It flashes, and a text shows up on it. I can talk, and when whoever it is talks back to me, it texts me, and I read it."

Angel looked at her. "Who is your doctor? I've been having problems with my ears. I think I have too much sand in them."

"I thought you were leaving tomorrow for your island."

"Yes, but I have a home here a little way down the beach," Angel said.

"Do you? Are you moving back here?" Emily asked.

"Eventually. Now, what was your doctor's name?" Angel asked again.

I had never seen Angel talk to a woman like this. He's usually trying to get them into bed. I better write down this doctor's name also. It never hurts to have a spare pair of hearing aids. Angel treats Emily like she is his sister, and he hugged her and told her not to worry so much.

"Doctor Turley. He is so kind. You'll really like him."

I smiled at Emily. "I'm sure we will. So, the hearing aids you gave away are the pair someone ordered and didn't pick up. So, Dr. Turley gave them to you," I asked.

"I told you he was kind," she replied.

"Yes, you did. You're lucky to have such a kind ENT. I will most definitely visit him." *I'll order a pair and have her doctor give them to her.*

"So, tell me what happened when you were almost run over," I said, looking into her beautiful eyes.

"It was bizarre. It gives me the chills just thinking about it. We went to the grocery store because we were out of milk. I swear I forget how fast kids can go through a gallon of milk. Now I buy two gallons at a time." Angel chuckled, and I rolled my eyes. This might take a while.

"Anyway, I got out of the van to run in and get some milk. Jason was staying in the car with the kids. I stepped onto the sidewalk and heard a noise. When I turned around, a car drove onto the sidewalk and came straight at me. I swear they stepped on the gas pedal. I jumped out of their way, and my head hit the sidewalk. I actually had to touch their car to help me jump.

"I knew my hearing aids fell out. But I was too shaken up

to hunt for them. I wasn't thinking. Jason jumped out of our vehicle to help me, and I was too scared they would come back and run him over, so I got back into our vehicle and left without our milk and my hearing aids. When my brain started working again, I returned to find my hearing aids, but when I found them, they were unwearable."

I looked at Angel and could tell he thought the same thing I did. Someone had tried to run over Emily on purpose. Who could want to harm her? I decided not to say anything to her; there was no use in scaring her since nothing else had happened. I figured it was a one-time thing. She was fortunate she had her hearing aids on at the time.

"That must have been scary."

"It was. All of us were shaking on the way home. I don't know what would happen to the kids if something happened to me," she said, shaking her head. "That's when I realized I had to make sure I was careful with what I did in my life. What if I broke my leg or something? It would hurt all of us. Jason helps me a lot, but he's a kid who deserves to have some fun in his life."

"Then why would you give your hearing aids away? Don't you realize that if you hadn't had your hearing aids in, they would have run over you? If something happened to you, where would the kids go?"

"They would go to Maggie's cousin. That's who tried to take them from me until they found out my dad didn't have life insurance. Those people are not good. My friend from college is an FBI agent. She did a background check on the guy and found out he went to jail for beating his ex-wife. They've dealt in drugs and all kinds of scary things," she explained.

"I don't want the kids anywhere around them. By the

way, I need to be going. I swear, once I start talking, I can go on forever. I'm sorry for blabbering. Thank you for everything."

I watched as she walked next door and inside her house.

"She's perfect," Angel said.

I looked over at Angel. "What do you mean?"

"Well, she loves kids, and she can cook. Her home is cozy, and it makes me want to stay there and take a nap. And she's a great cook."

"You already said that. So, ask her out."

"She's not perfect for me. She's perfect for Matt."

"Are you kidding me? She isn't perfect for Matt. And don't call him up and tell him about her."

"I already did. Matt told me not to try to set him up on any dates," Angel said, laughing.

"Good for him. Now I have to leave. I'm meeting my mom for lunch."

"I'll see you later. I think I'll walk down and look at my house."

"Do you want me to go with you?"

"No, I'm big enough to go there on my own. I don't understand why you think I need you to hold my hand. It's been two years since Dory died. I can walk into my house without breaking down," Angel declared.

"I never thought differently. I only made a suggestion." I could have kicked myself as soon as it came out of my mouth. I knew Angel was past that time in his life. But I remembered how torn up he was when his girlfriend, Dory, drowned in the ocean. Angel hadn't lived in his home since that day. I didn't care what he said; I knew that was why he hadn't returned.

10

EMILY

WHEN I REACHED OUT TO MY ENT, HE INFORMED ME HE HAD a pair of hearing aids available for monthly payments. I was so excited, I rushed over to pick them up.

"What happened to your previous hearing aids?" he asked.

"I gave them to a teenager who needed them more than I did. Jason mentioned they're working really well for him."

Curious, he inquired, "I would like his name. If he's going to wear hearing aids, I need to examine his ears."

"He doesn't have money for that, so you'll have to offer him a free exam."

"I can certainly do that. If you can get me his number, I can set up an appointment for him to come and see me." He paused looking at me intently. "Emily, you can't simply give away your hearing aids. With five kids, you need to have your hearing aids on all the time."

Emily acknowledged, "You're absolutely right. I just felt sorry for the boy. You know how kids used to made fun of me when I was young. Jason said they did the same to that boy. He told me the poor kid cried when he heard Jason talking. He was so excited he ran home right to share the good news with his mom."

"I won't charge him anything. I'll tell him the exam comes with the hearing aids," he assured her, "

"Thank you. I told Jason to tell him those were my spare hearing aids. I've been telling my friends how kind you are. But now, I need to get back home; I have two dinners to prepare for tonight. I've started my own catering business."

"You have? Can I give your phone number to my wife? We have a wedding coming up in two months. She'd love to have you cater it. She still raves about the food from the restaurant in Colorado where you were chef."

"Of course, I would love to get together with her and talk about what she wants for dinner. Who's getting married?" I inquired.

"Our daughter. I'm sure she'd like to speak with you too."

"I look forward to it." My mind was rushing with thoughts about potential income I could make if I started catering weddings.

I could barely hold in my glee as I picked up Kelsey from the chair she sat in and walked out of my doctor's office. I might have to hire servers if I start doing weddings. I could even make the cake. I had years of experience making wedding cakes. That's what I did when I first graduated from culinary school. I went to the wedding warehouse and bought two wedding cake books.

Then, we stopped at a thrift store to check their selection of pans. I had some, but I needed more. "You're getting ahead of yourself, Emily," I reminded myself, taking a deep breath to slow down. Suddenly, I hit the jackpot—more cake books for just a dollar each. When I spoke to the girl at the counter, she mentioned they would be receiving more wedding items soon. The woman who used to bake wedding cakes in town had passed away, and her family donated everything.

"I believe Joseph said there were tons of pots and pans."

"THAT'S WONDERFUL. Do you know what day they'll arrive?"

"Wednesday is the day they bring more stuff into the shop. Give me your phone number, and I will call you."

"You will! Why, that's incredibly kind of you."

"My cousin is Marcus Knight, the young man you gave your hearing aids to."

"Oh, don't tell him about that. I got a new pair today. My doctor wants to see Marcus for a check-up. It won't cost him anything. Could I get his phone number?"

"Sure, that's wonderful. Here's his number. I'll see you on Wednesday morning. We open at nine, but if you come at eight, I can let you in early."

"What's your name?" I asked.

"Lori Knight."

"Lori Knight, it is an honor to meet you."

"You too."

"This is Kelsey. She's my baby sister."

"Yes, I know Kelsey. I used to sit with the kids when Maggie and your dad would go out to dinner together. I think what you are doing is so wonderful. It was such a horrible accident. We lost six people who lived here in town."

"Yes, it was terrible. I'm happy I was able to take my brothers and Kelsey. I love them so much. If you ever have spare time, would it be alright if I called you? I think I'm going to need help with the weddings.

"Yes, call me any time. If you need more help, I know

some of my friends are looking for work. Any time you need me to come over and be with the kids, please call me."

"I'll definitely take you up on that. Could I please get your number too?"

I walked out of that thrift store humming. I could hear Kelsey's chatter in her own words She kept the name Mac, and it made me smile—I was finally catching the break I needed to provide for my family, and now I could even afford new shoes for everyone.

I almost skipped down the sidewalk until I saw that car again. It was very recognizable. Its purple hue with white stripes down the hood was unmistakable. I hurried to the van, buckled Kelsey in, then ran to the driver's side. Taking no chances, I quickly snapped a couple of photos with my phone.

Did they intentionally try to run me over? It certainly seemed so; the car had mounted the sidewalk. Was I being specifically targeted? Why would someone be after me? "Stop it, Emily," I chided myself. "You're imagining things again. Just go home and relax with your magazines."

Still, I kept glancing in the rearview mirror, half expecting to see the car trailing me. Although it wasn't visible, an eerie feeling lingered that I was being followed. As I turned onto our beachside road, sure enough, the car sped past.

I made a quick U-turn, hoping to capture the license plate with my camera—a detail I regretted not capturing earlier in the parking lot. Panic gripped me, and I pulled over to calm myself with deep breaths. I looked back at Kelsey, who had fallen asleep amidst the chaos

I headed home to put the baby to bed and start cooking. I promised myself I would always look around to see if that car was anywhere near us, and I would call the police if necessary.

Back home, while I nearly finished cooking dinner, I realized I had forgotten to cook the rice, and time was tight. I had to deliver these meals to my clients within the hour. I hurriedly served the kids' dinner; Jason took over feeding Kelsey while I rushed to cook the rice. I scolded myself internally, 'Focus, Emily. You can't afford to mess up these dinners. People pay well for your cooking. I was so happy I found that butcher who had the best meat.

There was a knock on the door. Jason was going to answer, and I stopped him. "Jason, make sure you look who it is first."

"Okay."

"Hi, Jason."

"Hey, Kash, come on in."

I watched as my sexy, hot neighbor walked to where I stood, putting the food in the containers. *Should I mention the car incident? No, I don't think I will. It might all be my over-active imagination.* I almost leaned into him for a kiss sensing an unusual connection between us. I thought he was going to kiss me. What is wrong with me?

"Hello, Kash. How are you?"

"I will be going out of town for a week or two. I'm not sure. I was supposed to take Max with me, but I had to cancel. I can take him to the kennel..."

I didn't let him finish. "No, we'll watch him. We love having him here. When are you leaving?"

"Tomorrow morning."

"Leave him here tonight. We have to deliver my dinners, but we'll be right back."

"How about I stay here while you and Jason deliver the food."

"Yes!" Tommy shouted.

"Umm, I don't know. Do you know how to babysit?"

"What's to know. Just change Kelsey's diaper before you go, and everything should be fine."

"Okay, come on, Kelsey, let's change your diaper. Thank you so much, Kash!"

DELIVERING the food with the younger kids at home made it much easier. I was able to go through everything on the menu without rushing because the younger kids were in the car. When we headed back home, I looked at Jason. "Do you mind helping me deliver the dinners?"

"NO, I wish I could help you with more things. Like maybe you could teach me to cook, and eventually, I could help you with that too."

"OH, Jason, I would love that. You'll be an amazing cook. I might be catering a wedding. If I do, I'm hoping I get to make the cake."

"I SAW THOSE MAGAZINES. I went through them and saw some cool cakes. Baking cakes would be awesome."

"WE ARE GOING to be the best catering service around. We'll have to come up with a name for our business."

. . .

"Our business?"

"Well, sure, this is a family business."

"Thank you. You're the best sister ever."

"Hey, I feel so blessed to have you for my brother. I'm sorry I didn't visit you guys more often."

When we pulled into the driveway, I felt like Jason and I were a little closer. Inside, we found Kelsey had her pajamas she was in Kash's arms, both of them peacefully dozing in the recliner. Damn, I couldn't breathe. I wanted to cry. Would I ever find someone to love me?

I knew I wouldn't have anyone for a lot of years to come. 'Oh well, Stop feeling sorry for yourself and think about what you do have,' I admonished myself, shaking my head and smiling.

This was the man who didn't want kids living next door to him. If he could change that fast, then anything was possible. Max was asleep by the chair. I reached down to take Kelsey out of his arms, and he startled awake. When he opened his eyes, they gazed into mine—his were the bluest I'd ever seen. He smiled, and I couldn't help but smile back.

"I better head on home. It's past my bedtime," he murmured.

"Thank you. It was so much easier with the kids being here at home," I replied.

"You're welcome."

After he left, I realized I was starting to develop feelings for Kash Walker. I needed to be more cautious; I was nothing like the women he usually brought home. I wasn't a stalker, but sometimes the gate was open, and I saw them. They would be lounging by the pool or slow dancing on the deck, rarely the same woman more than three times.

Maybe I'll start a diet tomorrow, perhaps intermittent fasting. It might help me shed some weight from my curves if I didn't eat until noon. I'm glad my waist is tiny—at least I have that going for me. I wish my breasts were smaller, but you can't have everything. At least they are firm. That's something, I guess.

I laughed at myself as I crawled into bed. I needed to get my thoughts from the irresistible Kash Walker.

11

KASH

I couldn't stop thinking about Emily as she loaded the kids into the car and delivered her dinners to her clients. She was stunningly beautiful, and I doubted she even realized it. She rarely wore makeup, and honestly, she didn't need to. Her eyes radiated warmth and amusement, almost as if they were lit from within.

Even when she attempted to stifle a laugh, her eyes betrayed her, twinkling with mirth. And those exquisite lips... I found myself daydreaming about kissing and savoring those luscious, red lips. I had to stop dwelling on her gorgeous figure and enticing curves. I could imagine making passionate love to her all night long, and I was certain that day would come.

I'd decided to stop bringing other women home; they couldn't distract me from my thoughts of Emily. For now, I resolved to not rush things but to gradually become her friend and integrate into her life. It was clear my dog Max adored her, and her entire family seemed quite fond of him as well. Now, my challenge was to make her fall in love with me. Was this really what I wanted?

My thoughts were interrupted by Matt's voice. "Damn it, Kash, did you hear anything I just said?"

"Sorry, no, I didn't catch that."

"You'll end up in an accident if you keep daydreaming like this. What's on your mind?"

"My neighbor."

"The one with all those kids? Did your mom tell her she has to leave because you didn't want kids living next door?"

"No, I don't mind them living there. They're good kids and very quiet. I have their sister Emily on my mind."

"Oh, I see. Tell me about her."

"Her name is Emily Jones, and well, she's incredibly attractive."

"Stop right there. Don't say another word. What you need is a woman. That name does sound familiar," Matt remarked with a shrug

"No, I don't need a woman. I've tried that route, and it didn't work."

"Have you already slept with Emily?"

"Hell no, not even close. I haven't even kissed her, though I certainly intend to. The first chance I get to kiss those plump red lips, I won't hesitate." I haven't even brushed up against her. Why does saying that stir up such intense desire in me? I don't know, but I can't get her out of my mind. "I'm sure she tolerates me because of Max; he's my dog, but he loves the baby, Kelsey. They adore each other."

"Max! Do you let that crazy dog near a baby?"

"They don't want to be separated. He's staying with Emily and the kids right now."

"How many kids does she have, exactly?"

"Five, they're her siblings, not hers."

"True, but she's raising them. You could never live with five kids. What about when you two have your own? That'd be like eight kids in your house. When would you find time for each other? There wouldn't be any spontaneous afternoon naps or hours of passionate sex. She'd be too exhausted even for nighttime intimacy."

"You're getting way ahead of yourself, Matt. I never said I was getting married, and I damn sure didn't say I wanted to have kids right now. Relax and take a deep breath. It's as if you're planning my whole future for me. I'm not discussing Emily with you anymore. I can't explain how I feel when I'm still trying to figure it out myself. Now, who are we meeting?"

"Sorry, I can't picture you in love. Have you ever been in love before?"

"No, and I'm not in love now. I don't know if I will ever be, so let's drop this conversation. I'm not discussing Emily with you anymore. I can't tell you how I feel if I don't know myself. Now, who are we meeting?"

"We're meeting Jax. He said there are two people we are taking with us. He'll provide the details when he arrives."

"Is he staying here in Afghanistan? It sounds like he's waiting for trouble to catch up with him."

"You know Jax, he thrives on this stuff. He mentioned there are more Americans here. He said they were scared and hiding somewhere in a bunker. He's determined to find them and bring them home."

"Here he comes. Who does he have with him?"

"I am not taking her with us."

"Calm down. I'm sure she doesn't want to see you either."

I looked at my old friend. "Hello, Lara."

"Kash, my God, you get better looking every time I see you."

I pulled Lara in for a hug. She ignored Matt. "I didn't know you were still here working."

"I was a captive, but Jax saved me. This little guy is Tony. He's traumatized because he witnessed his family being killed right before his eyes. They would've killed him too if I hadn't dashed out of hiding and grabbed him. I'm taking him to his grandparents, who live in the United States."

I watched as Lara finally looked at Matt. "Hello, Matt."

"Lara. Let's get going. Jax, why don't you come home for a while? I'm sure your family misses you."

"I'll go home when I get these other people out. If you see my dad, will you tell him I'll see him soon?"

"I will. Stay safe."

"Goodbye, Lara, Tony. I'll see you when I return to America, okay."

The little guy had a faraway look on his face, clearly shell-shocked. I'd seen that look many times. We boarded the plane, and I went to the cockpit and started the aircraft. After we were in the air, Matt joined me.

"I didn't know those fuckers held Lara captive. I would've stormed in and gotten her out in a heartbeat. I know she no longer loves me, but I still wouldn't have let her sit in that fucking prison."

"I know. Are you alright?"

"Yeah, it's the first time I've seen her since she told me to go fuck myself. I didn't know she was still here." I felt him staring at me. "I'm going to give you some advice, Kash. Don't ever let yourself fall in love because your heart will be ripped out and cut into tiny pieces. Then, while trying to figure out what happened, you'll be stabbed in the back by someone you thought was your friend," Matt said.

"What is she doing?" I asked.

"I believe they are both sleeping. Forget what I said. I wasn't in love. I'm just feeling sorry for myself."

I chuckled, letting him think I believed him. But I remembered when Lara broke up with him. Matt had no clue why she did it. I could still see the shock and hurt on his face. I remembered how he was after their breakup. He drowned his sorrows in alcohol for two months until we convinced him to get his act together.

Lara West was a reporter, always seeking out trouble spots. She gravitated towards countries in perpetual conflict, and Matt and Lara were a couple deeply in love, or so we all thought. Until one day, she ended it with him. He never saw it coming and never understood why. She refused to discuss it with him. After their breakup, she disappeared for six months, and no one knew where she went.

As we disembarked from the plane, Lara asked if she could stay at my place for a couple of weeks. I hesitated briefly, not wanting Emily to get the wrong idea. But Lara was my friend from wartime. "Of course, you can. Do you want to ride back with me?"

"Yes, thank you."

12

EMILY

I thought I heard a car outside, and then I saw Max's tail wagging. Kash must be home. Glancing out the window, I spotted Kash carrying a child inside his house. A woman with long red hair stepped out of the vehicle, her hair pulled back in a ponytail, slinging an old duffle bag over her shoulder. She looked weary, and then it hit me—it was Lara West. With a big grin on my face, I rushed to the front door, flinging it open just as Lara tossed her bag aside and sprinted towards me. We screamed in delight before embracing each other tightly.

I couldn't believe my best friend was here. "What are you doing here? I've been trying to locate you for a year."

"I'm sorry, I've been in Afghanistan. I couldn't use a phone; I couldn't take the chance of someone finding me. I've been in hiding, then I was captured and held prisoner for a while. Jax saved me. What are you doing back here in Maine?"

"Let me show you, come inside." We entered the house, and three of the kids were there; the other two came walking in from outside. "These are my brothers, and the baby there is my sister." I knew it dawned on her that I was now raising my siblings. She wiped away a tear.

"They are beautiful, just like their older sister. I'm sorry for your loss." Lara sniffed. "I'm sorry I wasn't here for you when you needed me. What the hell happened?"

"There was an accident on the freeway. I knew you were somewhere dangerous having fun filming a war. Why were you still in Afghanistan?"

"Because there are so many Americans still trying to get out. Did you see the little boy Kash carried into his house? He saw his entire family murdered. I hid him. His grandparents will be here tomorrow to pick him up."

"That's heartbreaking. It's unfathomable that people still live like that in this day and age. Poor little guy."

"I've missed talking to you. We'll catch up after I get some sleep."

"Yes, I'm so happy to see you. I'll tell you everything later."

"I can't believe you're here."

"How do you know Kash?"

"We met during foreign deployments years ago. Kash specializes in rescuing people, and this time, I was the one in need. He's friends with Matt."

"Oh, how is that working out with Matt's friend?"

"It's okay. I saw him. I'm over that cheating Matt Grey. Let's not talk about him. I'll be back."

"I'll see you later."

"So, you know Emily?"

"Yeah, she's my best friend. I didn't know about her dad and stepmother dying. Poor kids. Poor Emily. My God, she must have her hands full."

"Emily did what she had to do. She would do it again in the blink of an eye," I replied.

"So, you and Emily know each other pretty well," Lara remarked, looking at me.

"No, she's lived here for eight months, but we don't know each other that well. She watches Max for me when I'm away. The baby absolutely loves Max."

"You still hanging out with those brainless, long-legged women?"

"They are not brainless. Right now, I'm not hanging out with anyone. What about you? Who do you hang out with since you broke Matt's heart?"

"I'm not going to answer that. Where can I sleep?"

"Follow me. There are towels in the bathroom, and you can start a load of laundry whenever you need to. I know you probably didn't have access to a washer and dryer where you were."

"Thank you. I can't wait to wear clean clothes. Do you have a spare T-shirt I could borrow? I'll start a load right away."

I went into my room and stripped off my clothes, jumping in the shower. I hadn't pictured Lara and Emily as best friends; they were two completely different people. I should have gotten Max before taking my shower. Dressed in an old pair of sweats, I headed into the backyard to fetch Max. When he saw me, he ran to me—the traitor had missed me.

I knocked on the door to thank Emily for taking care of Max. "Hello, Emily."

"Hi, Kash. I see you found Max."

"Thank you for taking care of him. I was gone longer than expected."

"No problem; don't worry about it. So, Lara mentioned

that you rescue people in other countries. Or is it only Afghanistan?"

"We go where we are needed."

"My brother is missing overseas. He's twenty-seven and disappeared three years ago."

"I'm sorry to hear that. What was your brother doing overseas?"

"He joined the Marines when he graduated from high school. I begged him to go to college, but he said he wanted to be a Marine. He was in Iran. We wrote to each other weekly, but he stopped writing three years ago. My dad brushed it off, thinking he'd show up eventually. He refused to help me find him.

My dad put it off on Maggie, saying his wife told him they couldn't afford to hunt for Graham. The Marines only said that he was missing in action. I saved up to hire someone to help me, but then the accident happened. Lara has been looking for him, but she hasn't had any luck. I went overseas as a reporter for six months, trying to find any leads. Then they found out I wasn't a real reporter, and I had to leave."

I couldn't picture Emily overseas in Iran hunting for her brother. "I'll see if I can find out anything for you. What's his name?"

"Franklin Graham Jones. We call him Graham."

"I'll see if I can find anything out about him for you."

"Thank you."

I nodded and turned and was about to leave when Emily stopped me. I had to get out of there quick, or she would be able to tell I had an erection. That outfit she wore was about the sexiest thing I'd seen in a while—a mini dress with spaghetti straps that clung to her like a second skin.

"I packed you and Lara and the child some dinner." I

heard a vehicle pull up in the front of the house. We walked to the front and Lara was hugging an older man and woman. Lara had my tee-shirt on and a pair of shorts that she held up with one hand. "That must be the grandparents."

"Yes, I'm sure it is. They arrived early. Goodbye, Emily."

"Bye."

I walked to the front yard and wondered what Emily thought about Lara wearing my clothes. I wish she would have worn the robe that I gave her. Why do I even care? Dang, I forgot my dinner. I turned around and called out to her before she went back inside the house. "Emily, I forgot our dinner." She laughed and handed me a tray with dinners all made up in containers. "Thank you. I'm starving."

"You're welcome."

13

EMILY

"Wow, these look absolutely delicious. How many different types of cakes did you prepare?"

I glanced at Lara, as she sampled another bite of some cakes I baked. I offered her a warm smile. "Well, the bride and groom are coming here this evening to sample the cakes and see what flavor they want. So, I've baked four different kinds."

"Oh, I really enjoyed the carrot cake, but the lemon is delicious too. But my favorite is the carrot cake with the vanilla buttercream frosting. I don't know how the couple is going to choose. They are all so good. I think I'm going to take a nap. I didn't sleep at all last night."

"Why don't you talk to me about it? Sharing your thoughts might help," I suggested.

"It's those nightmares from my time in captivity with the Taliban. Every time I close my eyes, those dreadful rats come back to haunt me. I can't sleep because I'm afraid if I close my eyes, they'll bite me. There were so many rats in that place. I believe the Taliban put them there on purpose.

You could hear men screaming as the rats attacked them at night."

"Is that what happened to you? Were the rats all over you?"

"They would wake me up at night when they bit me. I tried to block all the holes, but they just chewed through everything. I'm planning to take some time off to deal with these nightmares."

"That makes me so angry that they held you there. I wish you would stop going to those countries. Are you trying to get killed?"

"You know as long as there are conflicts of war, I will be there. This is my job. I want to show the world what is happening in those countries. But like I said I am considering taking some time off. My newspaper threatened to lay me off if I didn't take a break. I've been thinking about freelancing, which might not be a bad idea. Other newspapers have offered me positions, so that an option."

"You could give the freelancing a try, and if you don't like it, I'm sure you can find a job anywhere you want. You'd probably even triple your pay if you freelance."

"That's a possibility. Well, I'll catch you later."

"Here, take this cake to Kash."

"What's the deal with you and Kash?"

"Nothing, we are just neighbors."

"But you feed him. Do people usually feed their neighbors or is it just you?"

"What? Oh my God. Do you think he thinks I'm coming on to him by feeding him? Oh, brother, I don't want him to g. Let me see that cake. Can you wait here with the kids while I go over? It'll only take a minute." Without waiting for Lara's response, I rushed out through the back door, heading to Kash's house via his backyard. I knocked on the screen door, anxiously awaiting his response.

"Hello," he said from behind me. I almost dropped the cakes.

"Uh, hello," I said as I turned around.

"Are these for me?"

"Yes, I have a couple coming to try samples for their wedding. I thought you would like some cake. But Lara was concerned that you might misunderstand my intentions. I want to be hospitable, but I don't want it to be misconstrued..."

"No, I don't think that at all."

"I don't want you to think I'm trying to buy your affection by feeding you." I thought he'd burst out laughing, but he held it in even though his eyes held a hint of laughter.

"Well, I just wanted you to know because Lara commented. She said neighbors don't feed each other. I wanted you to know because I always have a surplus of food around the house, and, quite frankly, I enjoy feeding you because you like my cooking. Well, what do you have to say?"

He looked at me like he wanted to say something, so I stood there staring into his beautiful eyes, waiting. Then he kissed me. He just bent his head and locked his lips with mine. He even teasingly sucked on my bottom lip, for Christ's sake. Before he stood back, he took the cakes from my hands and pulled me onto the screened-in porch. He set the cake on the table and kissed me again.

"That's what I've been craving. I wanted to taste your lips."

"You have. How come?"

"Because your lips look irresistible, everything about

you looks delicious. If we could get a babysitter, we could have some time to do more tasting."

"More tasting. What do you mean?"

He backed me up against the wall and held me close. "Can you feel what I mean now?"

Boy, could I. His arousal pressed against me, sending a rush of sensations straight to my core, causing my panties to grow damp. I pulled his head down and kissed his lips, one long passionate kiss.

His hands were under my blouse. He held my oversized breast in his hand, playing with the nipple. I wanted to get naked with him. Then I remembered I had too much to do. I couldn't play house with Kash, right now. I had too much responsibility, five of them, and they would always come first. So, I pushed away.

"I'm sorry, I can't do this. There are five reasons, and they are waiting for their lunch. Goodbye. I took a deep breath and held it for a second before letting it out. "Your lips taste good too. If I could, I would love nothing better than to get naked with you, but I can't."

I WAS LEFT SPEECHLESS, unable to move due to my intense arousal. When she glanced back at me, I flashed a grateful smile. "Thanks for the cakes, Emily, and one of these days, you and I will be together. So, you might want to put that on your schedule. Oh, and I love it when you feed me." As soon as she departed, I went straight to the shower, taking a cold one to cool down. It was a myth; cold showers did nothing to quell my desires.

Grabbing a shovel I headed to my backyard. I was determined to create a garden of my own after seeing Emily's. I went and bought a bunch of wood and dirt from Lowes. While I was there, I got a lot of information on how to do this. But something wasn't right; I stood there looking at the wood like it would build itself.

"What are you doing?" A voice interrupted my thoughts, and I looked up to see Emily's brother, Jason, watching me.

"I'M TRYING to build a garden with this wood," I admitted.

"So, are you planning to make a container garden, or do you want a garden with the wood frame around it?"

"I thought I would build it up using wooden boxes, similar to what Emily has."

"I can help you with that," Jason offered, swiftly rearranging the wood as if he knew exactly what he was doing.

"We can help too," Tommy said.

"Great, you three can sort all the nails and screws. I have cans filled with them; my mom gave them to me after my dad passed away."

"Were you sad when your dad died?" one of the little boys asked, and I knew I had to respond honestly, because these little guys lost both their parents.

"I was so sad. I wasn't ready for my dad to leave. I was angry at everyone for a while, and then I was just sad. I was fourteen, and I cried for a week straight. I'm still sad. I miss my dad every day."

"I'm sad too. I miss my mom and my dad. But mostly my mom." I saw a tear roll down his cheek. I bent and wiped it off.

"I'm sorry you lost your parents." I listened as they talked about their parents for thirty minutes. Emily had come by to check on them, and I told her they were helping me. Jason was a wiz at DIY. His bangs kept flying into his eyes and he would push them away. We had planter boxes built and the dirt put in them; now, all I had to do was buy my plants.

"Wow, look at what we did, Jason. I couldn't have gotten this finished without your help, and to be honest, I probably wouldn't have gotten started. So, I owe all of us a pizza dinner. Ask your sister when a good day for a pizza night would be."

"Saturday or Sunday would work. Emily takes those days off until we start catering for weddings. Emily said most people get married on Saturdays."

"Yeah, I guess they do. So how is the catering business going?"

"It's busy. Emily is cooking a lot now. She's teaching me to cook so I can help her more."

"You're a good brother, Jason." Then I looked at the little guys. "Thank you so much for helping, boys. I finally managed to separate all my nails."

"I like you," four-year-old Mikey said as he climbed onto my lap where I sat on the lawn furniture. Before I knew it, he had snuggled up and wrapped my arm around him.

"Mikey is sleepy. We always know when he gets tired, he has to have someone's arm around him. I'll take him home to Emily," Jason said.

"Thank you, boys, for helping me. Maybe we can play some basketball sometimes when you're not busy."

"Sure."

"Do you have to work tonight?"

Jason stopped and looked at me. "No."

"How about we go check some plants out at the nursery, then."

"Okay, I need to check with Emily first."

"Okay, I'll write down what I need to buy." I watched as

Jason carried his little brother inside their house, with the other two trailing behind. I wondered if I should back off with getting too involved with this family. Jason, Emily, and the baby walked into my backyard. I was still in the chair, and before I could get up, Kelsey climbed onto my lap.

"Kelsey, for crying out loud. Get off of Kash."

Kelsey shook her head. "No." I glanced at Emily, who was smiling and shaking her head. I couldn't help but chuckle. The baby looked into my eyes and planted a wet kiss on my cheek before curling up on my lap.

She glanced at me.

"I hear you're planning to buy some plants. I hope you don't mind, but I made a list of specific plants that are suitable for planting at this time of year. While you're there, I'll have Jason pick up some basil for me. It would be great if you planted some basil yourself, the smell is heavenly." Emily walked over to my new little garden. "Oh, this is an excellent spot to plant your garden. Come along, Kelsey. We need to head back home."

"No."

"That's her new favorite word. I've tried asking her not to say it, but she says it anyway. She's been ignoring me so far."

"She's just a baby. She'll go through a lot of favorite words. My friend Austin told me that when his baby started talking, he had to watch every word he said because she repeated everything."

"Oh, Lord, did you hear that, Jason? You'll have to let me know if I say something I shouldn't, and I'll do the same for you."

"I'm sure you'll be telling me more times than I tell you, Emily, you never say bad stuff except when that person tried running you over that time."

14

EMILY

I STILL FELT THE LINGERING SENSATION OF HIS KISS AFTER ALL this time. I had to force myself to go over and act as if nothing had happened. While talking to him, a powerful attraction coursed through me. My body responded, my nipples hardening at the memory of his touch, and my thoughts wandering to how hard his erection was. I had to leave before I embarrassed myself further.

I WALKED AS NORMALLY as I could, back to my yard, knowing he watched me. I bent down to pick up Kelsey so we could move faster. Why would someone like Kash be interested in me? I had just stepped into my yard when he called my name. I turned to face him.

"Yes."

"I promised the boys I would treat them to pizza. Is tonight good for you?"

"Absolutely. We all love pizza. The children like pepperoni, but I'm good with any pizza. We can eat in the backyard. I just made a gallon of strawberry lemonade."

. . .

"GREAT, we'll stop on the way back and pick it up."

I NODDED AND WALKED AWAY. I needed to regain my composure and stop entertaining the thought that someone might want me. I'm a thirty-one-year-old woman raising five kids. I can't afford to let my hopes soar. My life was already overflowing with responsibilities for the foreseeable future.

When the phone rang, I answered it without looking at the name. "Hey, Emily. It's me, Lara."

"Where are you?"

"I'm going back to Afghanistan. The babies are dying over there. They are all starving. I wanted to let you know I've decided to start freelancing."

"Are you out of your mind? It's too dangerous for you to go back there so soon."

"I'm taking a cameraman with me. I'll make sure everyone can see what is going on. Babies are starving; I have to do something."

"You be careful."

"I will. Can you let Kash know where I've gone? I like having the Rangers know what is going on. Don't worry about me. I won't get caught this time. I bought a black wig. I'm going to blend in with the people of Afghanistan."

"Lara, I think this is one of the worst ideas you've ever had."

"If I think I'm in over my head, then I'll leave right away."

"I'll tell Kash, but he won't like it. You know he'll contact Matt."

"Matt means nothing to me. There is no Matt. Don't

forget he cheated on me. I still have those photos, and I'm going to keep them. If that bastard ever confronts me to ask why I broke up with him, I'll show him the pictures. But he knows why I broke up with him, that's why he never asked. Besides, it's been two years. I'm over Matt Grey."

I knew she would never get over Matt; her love for him was unwavering. "Please watch your back? You're my best friend, and I love you."

"I promise I'll be careful. Goodbye, Emily."

"Goodbye, Lara. Keep in touch if you can."

"I will if possible. I have to go."

Kelsey walked into the kitchen and rushed toward me. I picked her up and held her close. Tears welled up in my eyes. I loved this baby so much. I felt so bad that Maggie didn't have a chance to see her children grow up. I swore right then that I would show these kids how much I love them.

"Are you okay?" Kash asked, entering the kitchen with my basil.

"I'M SORRY, yes I'm fine. I feel so bad that Maggie won't see her children become adults. I love them so much. It scares me. What if I don't know how to be a good parent?"

"YOU ALREADY KNOW what to do. Why are you questioning yourself now?"

"IT'S JUST that when Kelsey saw me, she ran into my arms, and it hit me how much I love her. Ignore me; I'm being silly."

. . .

"You're not being silly. Now come on, the pizza is getting cold."

I laughed and nodded, wiping my cheeks, and then headed outside, where the boys were enjoying their pizza. "This looks delicious. Thank you, Kash. I appreciate not having to cook tonight."

"Tell me about the kid's other relatives? Jason mentioned they once tried to take him and the others away from you."

"That was when they thought our father left an insurance policy. They claimed that Maggie had told them there was a substantial life insurance policy. If anything happened to our father, she said she and the kids would be taken care of. But there was no policy, and the relatives went away."

"We didn't know them. Our mom never allowed them to visit our house. Our dad wouldn't let them visit us. I don't know when she would have spoken to them; it must have been over the phone. We'd never go anywhere with them," Jason said.

"It sounds suspicious that Maggie would mention it to her family without an actual policy. It doesn't sound like they were close," Kash said.

"Yes, I was surprised as well. When my mom passed away, there was an insurance policy. My father's lawyer told me he hadn't heard of a policy but would look into it. Regardless, it doesn't matter to me. I love my brothers and my sister. I would never let anyone take these kids from me. We belong together."

"I'd never live with anyone from my mom's family. She told me that her family was all crazy. That's why we never went to visit them," Jason replied.

Kash glanced at me. "You need to adopt them. You never know when something will come up."

"I don't have money for a lawyer," I replied, shaking my head.

Kash waved it off. "I'll have my friend talk to you. He can fill out the papers and submit them."

"Do you think I need to do something?" I asked with concern.

"I don't think you should take the chance that a policy won't show up," Kash said, biting into his pizza.

I looked at Jason. "What do you think?"

"Let's talk to Kash's friend. I don't want to take a chance that a court might side with them if that policy is out there somewhere. Because the last time I remember them yelling and saying they are a married couple and the courts will give us to them," Jason said.

"I agree. When can we talk to your friend?" I asked.

"I'll call Matt tonight," Kash said.

"Would that be Matt Grey?" I asked.

Kash nodded. "Yes, do you know him?"

"Yes, he hurt my best friend Lara, and she'll never get over that pain."

"Lara broke up with him," Kash replied.

"I'm not going to talk about Lara and Matt. He might not

want to speak to me. I may have called him something... Which reminds me, Lara went back to Afghanistan to report on all the children who were starving to death. I'm worried about her. She is a freelancer now because her newspaper wanted her to take a break." I turned my head and looked at Jason, "Do you want me to adopt you?"

"Yes. I want to make sure no one can take us away from you."

"I agree. We all have the same last name, so we don't have to worry about that."

15

KASH

I phoned Emily to informed her that Matt was coming by on Monday morning to talk to her. "He's bringing the necessary papers for you to fill out."

"Thank you. I'm eager to have all the paperwork sorted. I can't take the chance of someone trying to take the kids from me."

"I'll see you on Saturday."

"Okay, thank you so much for calling Matt for me."

I decided to take a step back from getting deeply involved with Emily and the kids. While I intended to maintain a friendly relationship, I didn't want to become so attached that it would be difficult for the children if things didn't work out.

Emily had her hands full with the kids and her new business, and I believed she needed time to settle into her new life. I planned to give her a few more months before asking her out. I had to go overseas in a week. I didn't know for how long. I'd leave Max with them. He was there most of the time anyway.

Moreover, Emily had seemed somewhat uneasy lately,

frequently appearing watchful and cautious. But when I inquired if something was wrong, she, assured me everything was good. Monday came fast. Matt was knocking at my door at seven in the morning.

"Don't you ever sleep?" I greeted Matt, who appeared as though he had been up for hours. When I pulled the door open, Matt stood there looking like he'd been up for hours.

"I have a ton of things I'm checking into at the moment. I need to talk with Emily. Do you think she's awake?"

"She's likely in the backyard enjoying her coffee before the kids get up.

"How do you know that?"

"I live next door, and sometimes I see her if I'm up early."

Matt began making his way to the backyard. "I'll head back there to see if she's around."

"So, you know Emily?"

"Yes, that's why I thought I heard her name, she had some choice words for me the last time we crossed paths. I think she blames me for Lara breaking up with me. She's Lara's best friend. I've dined at her restaurant, which, from what I hear, has lost most of its customers since she's left."

"Don't mention that to her. The last thing she needs is a guilty conscience. She told me Lara went back to Afghanistan to tell the world about the children who are dying from hunger over there."

I watched Matt's reaction closely and he was upset. I could tell he was angry. "Why does she take such risk with her life? I won't say a word to Emily about the restaurant."

"I'll walk with you." I heard Matt chuckle and decided to ignore him. "Hello, Emily."

"Good morning." I watched when she spotted Matt. I could tell she was still angry with him. "Hello, Matt. How have you been?"

"Hello Emily, I'm good. Kash explained everything to me about the kids. I'm so sorry for your loss. I guess this is one of your family members." We watched as Kelsey walked to me and held her arms up. I picked her up, and she kissed me. I grinned and kissed her back.

"Yes, this is Kelsey. Sweetheart, Kash is not going to carry you around. Now, come over here and have your breakfast."

I chuckled as I returned Kelsey to her breakfast spot, next to Emily. I could tell that Matt watched me. I was the guy who didn't allow kids to live next door. I always said they were noisy and messy. However, I had recently discovered the joy of being around children. "I'll leave you two to talk." Instead of heading home, I picked up Kelsey and her breakfast and walked into the kitchen. I could almost swear Matt's mouth was hanging open as he watched me walk away.

They talked for an hour before Emily walked back inside. "Thank you so much for watching Kelsey."

"You're welcome. I'll talk to you later. The boys are ready for school. I gave them cereal for breakfast."

"Thank you for your help."

As soon as I stepped back into my house, Matt started questioning me. "Is there something going on between you and Emily?"

"No, I'm waiting a few more months until her life gets settled more."

"She asked me what would happen to the kids if something happened to her. Did you know she almost got run down by a car? It drove up onto the sidewalk and tried to hit her. She said she thought it was a mistake at first, but then the same car started following her. She said it's gone by her house a couple of times. I suspect someone is stalking her."

"Why didn't she tell me this?"

"She doesn't want to trouble you with it. She was waiting for the person to stop following her. She believes it might be one of Maggie's relatives."

"I need to speak with her. If someone tried to run her over and is now following her, she should at least involve the police."

"She did contact the police, but they dismissed it as her imagination, even though she showed them the pictures she took with her phone."

"What? Damn it. I'm leaving for overseas next week, but before I go, I'm going to track down that car and find out why the hell he's following Emily."

"I'm not sure she wanted me to tell you anything. You know that lawyer-client confidentiality."

I glanced at Matt and shook my head. "Why wouldn't she want me to know about someone following her around?"

"Don't ask me. She barely spoke to me. I sensed she wanted to give me an earful about something. I could tell she was biting her tongue trying not to say anything. Emily has always been a quiet person. I remember Lara telling me that it worried her sometimes because Emily kept every-thing inside."

"Why did it worry her?"

"Lara told me once Emily only had her brother growing

up because their father didn't have a lot to do with Emily and Graham after he married Maggie."

"Yeah, that happens all the time after a parent remarries and has other children. Did you ever meet her brother?"

"I met him once when he was on leave. He was at Emily's place, and we went there for dinner. Does he still live around here?"

"No, he's missing in action. Emily mentioned he's been missing for three years. She told me she needed to know what had happened to him. I offered to look into it and see if I could find out anything. Lara has been trying to find out what happened to him as well."

Matt nodded thoughtfully. "Yes, now I remember. Emily still hasn't received any news about him. That doesn't sound promising. What do you think might have happened to him? I remember he went back to college while serving as a Marine, and eventually became an officer."

I looked at Matt. "I don't know. I hope I can find some answers for her so she can have closure if he died. I'll start calling around when I get back from overseas." I turned my attention to my friend, who had always kept his emotions concealed. He had been with Lara for at least three years before their breakup. "May I ask a personal question?"

"You can ask, but it doesn't mean I'll answer."

"Why did you and Lara break up?"

"That is something I'll never discuss. I've moved on, and I no longer let thoughts of Lara cause me pain. I need to get going. I'll see you next week; I'm joining you and Angel for the trip to Afghanistan."

"Angel is coming along? I thought he said he didn't want to go with us to Afghanistan?"

"He changed his mind. It suppose it gets pretty lonely on that island of his with no woman around to bother him. We all know women love Angel. He's reopening his house here back up. Hell, he's probably there already."

"Are you planning to walk down to his house?"

"I wasn't going to, but I guess I can. Would you like to join?"

"No. I'm going to talk to Emily and find out what's happening with that damn car."

"Now she'll probably hate me more for telling you about that car."

"She hates you already for breaking her friend's heart. No, matter how angry she is, she should've told me something."

"I'll catch you later." I waved as I made my way to Emily's house. I entered through the back door, and Max barked. "Do you ever stay home anymore?"

"Hi, Kash, how can I help you?"

"I want you to tell me everything you know about that car that has been following you. Matt has just informed me that it's the same vehicle that tried to run over you. I wish you had shared this with me, it sounds pretty important."

"Matt should have kept his mouth shut. He's my lawyer; he's not allowed to disclose what I tell him."

"He's concerned that someone is trying to harm you and he believes you're being stalked. I'm going to call one of my friends to come here and stay with you while I'm away."

"No, you are not." She even stomped her foot.

"Did you just stomp your foot? Why wouldn't you want someone to be here?"

"Because I can't allow you to take care of everything for us. I'm the grown-up in my family, it's my responsibility to take care of us. And yes, I might have stomped my foot."

"Alright, but if you change your mind, let me know."

"Okay, I will. We are having a small birthday party for

Kelsey; she's turning two tomorrow. Would you like to come over for cake and ice cream?"

"I would love to. What time should I be here?"

"Come for lunch, and afterwards we'll have cake and ice cream."

"I will see you at noon tomorrow." As I walked into my house, I dialed Marc Breaux, a Navy SEAL. "Hey, Marc."

"Kash, what's going on with you. Are you still involved in rescue missions?"

"Yes, I have a task for you, but it must stay discreet. My neighbor is having an issue with someone who tried to run her over. Now she's noticed the same car following her. We can't let her know I called you to watch out for her, or Emily will have a fit.

She is raising her younger siblings after her dad and stepmom were killed in an accident. So, I thought if you and young Adam want to spend some time on the Maine coast, we could tell her you are renting my place for a few weeks."

"That sounds good to me. I'll call Killian and let him know what is going on. When do you need me there?"

"Next Monday. You can introduce yourself, and that will be your opening to become nosey."

"You got it. I'll be there on Monday, bright and early."

"Thank you, Marc. She doesn't want me helping her, so I had to take matters into my own hands. Maybe she'll say something to you about the car."

"I'll do my best to extract information from her," Marc chuckled.

"Good, I don't know anyone better than you for getting information out of someone."

16

EMILY

I HEARD A KNOCK ON MY FRONT DOOR, AND MAX GROWLED. I had just managed to put Kelsey to sleep, and I had my list of cooking to do for tonight, so I hurried to answer the door before Kelsey woke up. A very handsome man stood there, tall and broad. I had to tip my head back to meet his gaze, which held the greenest eyes I had ever seen. He carried a sleeping little boy.

"It's usually best not to answer the door without checking who's on the other side, especially without a peephole," he remarked when I opened the door.

"You're absolutely right. Dang, I have to start remembering that. How can I help you?" I asked.

"I'm renting Kash's place for a few weeks, but I can't find his key. He said it would be under a pot, but it's not there. Do you happen to know where it might be?" he inquired.

"Wait a moment, I'll call him. I can't let you in without talking to him first." I picked up my phone and dialed Kash's number. He answered on the third ring. "Kash, there is a gentleman here who claims he's renting your house, but he can't locate the key. I hope this isn't your friend you wanted to keep an eye on me."

"That would be Marc. He's a retired Navy Seal; he needed to a break to unwind. I didn't hire him to watch over you. I told him the key under the pot in the backyard. Could you please put him on the phone?"

"I will, but he's holding a sleeping child in his arms," I replied

"Hello, Kash, sorry I had to bother your neighbor. Now that I know where the key is, I'll unpack my vehicle."

"Damn you're fast?" Kash replied.

"Yes, I am. Thank you. I'm sorry to bother you," Marc said, handing me back the phone.

"Why don't you lay your son on the sofa while you unload your vehicle?"

"Are you sure? That would help me a lot," he replied.

"Of course." I picked up Kelsey's blanket and spread it out on the sofa. As he walked in and laid the child down. Then he paused for a brief second. I knew what he was thinking, he must have been wondering to himself if I was a serial killer or a child kidnapper.

"I'm very trustworthy. We can leave the door open."

"Okay, thanks."

"I understand completely."

I watched as Marc kissed his son on the forehead, and then he left to unpack his vehicle. So, Kash lets service people stay at his place while he's gone. Kash has so many good qualities. I'm sure he also has plenty of women to keep him company. Not only am I ordinary, but I also have five kids. I knew after he kissed me, he regretted it. He hasn't tried anything since that day. Oh, well, that's my life.

"Thank you. I've unloaded my vehicle. It's incredible how much you have to pack when you have a child."

"He's very handsome."

"Thank you. Adam is my life," He said.

"I know what you mean," I replied.

"I thought you must have a child when I saw the baby blanket."

"I have five children. Kelsey is the youngest. She just turned two years old the other day."

"Wow, you look young for a mother of five kids."

I chuckled. "They are my siblings. My father and his wife died in an accident. I'm raising them."

"They are lucky to have you," he said.

"Thank you; I'm lucky to have them." Marc picked up his son and walked over to Kash's home. I'm glad someone will be close by if we need them.

It had been a week since Marc had been at Kash's home, and he had us over for a barbeque already. "Where did you learn to cook this good?" I asked, biting into a spare rib. "Did you make this sauce?"

"Yes. I learned everything from my dad. He was a great cook. He had a restaurant in New Orleans. He was known for his Cajun cooking."

"I bet everything he cooked was delicious. I might start adding Cajun food to my menu if I could get a few recipes from you, starting with this sauce. It's wonderful."

"Thanks, sure, I'll give you some recipes."

"What do you do?" I asked.

"I work with the Band of Navy Seals. We are a high-security bodyguard service. All of us are retired Navy Seals."

I turned my head and looked at him, "Did Kash ask you to watch over us?"

"Why would he do that? Are you in need of someone to watch over you?"

"I was almost run over on the sidewalk, but that was a

while back. After a while, I didn't worry about it, but now I've been seeing the same car following me around. It has me worried that maybe it's Maggie's crazy family."

"Who's Maggie?" he asked.

"She was my father's wife," I said.

"Why do you think it might be them?"

"When the accident first happened, they wanted the kids. I thought I was going to have a fight on my hands. Then they found out there was no insurance policy, and they stayed away. I don't know who the car belongs to; I thought it might be them."

"What did the police say?"

"They said they would patrol the area. I've never seen a police car drive by. I don't think they believed me."

"Hmm, would you mind if I looked into a few things? My buddy Ryes lives in town. What do you know about Maggie's family?"

"Not much at all. Jason would know more information; you can ask him some questions."

"Alright, I'll do that."

I listened as Jason shared details about Maggie's family with Marc. They were indeed crazy, at least two of her nephews had been to prison for robbery, and her sister got arrested for selling drugs. I was in shock. I needed to call Matt and tell him all of this. *I will never let those people around my family.* I wished for the millionth time that Graham was here to help me.

"I will gather all the information I can about these people. The more you know, the better it will be," Marc stated.

"Thank you, but this is your vacation time," I replied.

"I'm one of those people who always needs to stay busy."

"I know that feeling; I'm the same way."

∼

"HELLO," I said as I walked into the backyard and saw Emily and Marc sitting there like old friends.

"You're back early. Adam and I love your beach. Do we have to go home?" Marc asked with a chuckle.

I chuckled. "No, you can stay. We finished earlier than we thought. Angel and Matt are here too."

"Is Matt in the house?" Emily inquired.

"No, I'm right here."

"Matt, Marc has information about Maggie's family. We have to work on getting those adoption papers filed.

"I already filed them. But I'll take all the information you have."

I HEARD A LITTLE SCREAM, and Kelsey came charging at me. She ran and grabbed my legs. I laughed and picked her up; she kissed me and waited for me to kiss her back. It suddenly dawned on me that I loved this baby. I looked at the boys, and they ran over, bombarding me with questions. I saw Marc looking at me, and he smiled. *I've become close to these kids. How did this happen? These kids missed me as much as I missed them.* I glanced at Emily, wanting to pull her into my arms and keep her and the kids safe.

"Kash, do you have to go away again?" Jason asked, standing next to me.

"No, why? Do you four want to play a game of horse on the basketball court?"

"Yes!" they all shouted.

"Count me in. I'm on the kid's side," Angel said, crossing onto Emily's side of the yard.

· · ·

I COULDN'T BELIEVE Angel wanted to play basketball with us. That was a good sign. Maybe he wasn't drinking as much as I thought he was. We played for two hours, and the sun went down. Emily called the little guys in for their baths. I took Jason aside.

"If anyone ever tries to get into your house, you call me first, and then you call the police. I don't know if it will happen, but I want you to be aware. Here's a phone, keep it on you. It's yours."

"Jeez, thanks. I'm not sure if Emily will allow me to keep it."

"Tell her why I got it for you."

"Okay. Thank you."

"Hey, we'll finish this game tomorrow," I said, hugging him around the neck.

17

KASH

I carefully reviewed all the information Marc had provided, and it became evident that these people were trouble. I couldn't allow them anywhere near Emily or the kids. I was frowning when I looked at him. "Do you know where they live?"

Marc nodded, his expression serious. "They live in the mountains, about sixty miles from here. I did some investigation, and sure enough, there is a purple car there with white stripes down the hood parked there. So why didn't the police arrest the driver when the vehicle went up onto the sidewalk trying to kill Emily?"

I paced back and forth on the floor, seething with frustration that this bastard had not been arrested yet, and was now lurking around Emily and the children. "That's an excellent question. I'm going to find out why nothing has been done to help Emily. I'll visit the police department today and find out why no one initiated an investigation after Emily reported the incident. Did they ever open a case regarding the attempt to run over her?"

I shook my head in disbelief. The situation grew

stranger by the minute, and I became angrier, prompting me to head straight to the police department to demand answers.

An hour later, I found myself in front of the police chief's secretary. "Can I speak to someone in charge?" I inquired.

"I suppose so. Do you have an appointment?" she replied.

"All I want to do is ask a few questions," I said.

"Please have a seat, and I'll check if the chief can see you," she replied.

I sat down and waited for what felt like an eternity. I was determined not to leave without getting some answers, as it was high time someone got to the bottom of this. Thirty minutes passed, and I continued to sit and wait. I wouldn't budge; I needed to know the truth. Another half-hour elapsed before the chief finally emerged and asked how he could assist me.

"I want to know why someone hasn't been brought in for questioning in the case of the purple car trying to run over my friend months ago. Furthermore, why does no one do anything about it when she calls in and tells you that that same car has followed her to her house?" I demanded to know.

"I'm not sure what you're referring to. I deal with numerous cases every day. Annie, do you know what he's talking about?" the chief inquired.

"No, sir, I don't."

"I'm talking about Emily Jones's case. Nothing has been done since she reported the incident, and the vehicle has followed her. She reported this as well. Someone from your department assured Emily that a police car would patrol her neighborhood. But nothing has happened."

"Annie, retrieve that case for me. Why haven't I been informed of this?" the chief questioned.

"THERE IS NO FILE, sir. There must be a mistake," Annie replied.

"Emily wouldn't make a mistake like this. Someone within this office is connected to the Granger family, who have been harassing Emily. They attempted to kill her, and none of you helped her. Now the Army Rangers, Special Ops, and the Band of Navy SEALs are stepping in to help. I suggest you figure out who's erasing your files. We'll be there if the Grangers attempt anything against Emily and those five children again."

I noticed the chief's gaze on Annie, and by the look on her face, it seemed she might be facing some jail time or, at the very least, looking for another job soon. "If you find out anything, could you please let me know?" I handed him one of my cards and left the police station, determined to keep a close watch over Emily from this point forward. I made my way home; we had a basketball game to play.

I WATCHED my brothers playing basketball with Angel and Kash. They were having so much fun. I hated telling them we had to deliver dinners. "Boys, I hate to break this up, but we have to deliver the dinners to my clients now."

"Awe, do we have to?" Tommy protested, giving me a disappointed look.

"Yes, we do."

"Why don't the kids stay here with me? I can watch them," Kash offered.

"I'll help Emily," Jason said as he put his arm around me. "That way, our time will pass more quickly."

"Thank you, sweetie," I replied, grateful for Jason's support. I looked at Kash and hesitated, feeling like I might be imposing. "Thank you for the offer, but I think we can all go together. You're already doing so much for me, and I wouldn't want to become a burden or make you hide from us."

"You could never be a burden, and I will never hide from you. Kelsey can also stay, give her to me. She and I are best buddies."

"I'm not sure... I feel like I'm taking advantage of your kindness."

"Go ahead," he insisted

"Alright, thank you. Jason, help me load the car, then you can come back and continue your game."

"No, I want to go with you."

I looked at my brother, touched by his determination. "Are you sure?"

"Yes, we're a team."

I hugged him. "I'm sorry I moved away and hardly ever saw you. I would give anything to change that."

"Are you kidding? You lived in Aspen, Colorado. Who wouldn't want to live there?"

"I missed the beach," I confessed as I linked my arm with Jason, and we walked away.

I WATCHED both of them when they walked back into the house. Then I turned with Kelsey in my arms.

"You got it bad, buddy. What are you going to do?"

"I'll take it slow. Emily has already told me she has to

take care of her siblings and doesn't have time for a relationship. So, I'll be patient."

"Well, old buddy, I'm going to walk down to my place and check it out. I'll see you later."

"Yeah, I'll see you later. I looked at Kelsey. "Should I put you in your walker and play more basketball with your brothers."

She shook her head and said, "No." I chuckled.

"Alright, kids, come inside and I'll teach you how to play war."

"We already know how to play, Emily taught us."

"Well then, let's see who will win this game." We played until the boys started yawning. Emily came home.

"Thank you, Kash. I don't have to work tomorrow, so I want you to come to dinner. That is if you don't have plans."

"I don't have any plans."

"Great, then I'll see you for dinner. If any of your buddies are there, please bring them with you. Is Marc still here?"

"He's at Ash's tonight. But he'll be back tomorrow. I'll bring him, Adam, and Angel. Is that too many?"

"No, I'll make spaghetti and a salad. That'll be perfect."

18

KASH

I WAS WATERING MY PLANTS ON MY FRONT PORCH WHEN TWO police cars pulled into Emily's driveway. I turned off the water and made my way over. "What's going on?" I inquired as I approached them.

"We're here to speak with Emily Jones," one of the officers replied.

"I thought that was the reason for your visit. I'd like to know the purpose of your conversation with her," I added, wondering if this officer considered me foolish.

"Who are you?" the officer asked.

"I'm Kash Walker. Whatever you have to say to Emily, you can also share with me."

One of the officers elbowed his colleague. "This is the guy who spoke to the chief."

"We want to inquire about the incident involving a car that nearly struck Miss Jones on the sidewalk, as well as the vehicle that followed her here and drove past her house," the officer explained.

"So, you never found the report Emily filed. I suspect Annie got fired for tampering with that information."

"I can't discuss anything related to Annie with you or anyone else."

At that moment, Emily opened her door, and she and the children stepped outside. They halted when they saw the police talking to me. "Excuse me. Why are you on my doorstep?"

"We have some questions regarding the vehicle that attempted to run over you on the sidewalk," one of the officers replied.

"That was almost a year ago. I filed a report; can't you access it? I also made a report about the same car following me home. I'm sorry, but I need to get my kids to school. If you want to wait, you can. Why are there two police cars? Did they try to run over someone else?" Emily inquired.

"No, we couldn't locate the report. It'll only take a moment," the officer assured.

"A moment? Then I'm surprised two cars showed up," Emily retorted. She turned to me, "Can Kash tell you about it? I don't have time. Besides, you guys never did anything about it before."

"That's because Annie, the secretary, is seeing one of Maggie's family members, and she destroyed the reports," I said, looking at Emily.

"Wow, this is getting interesting. How did you find that out?" Emily asked.

"I went to the police department and asked them why they never patrolled your house, as they promised, but they had no record of your report."

"Can we finish this when I get back? I have to leave now."

"Yes, take them to school," I said. "We'll be in the back." She nodded and excused herself. Then Matt pulled into my driveway.

"Oh, there's my lawyer. I'm sure he'll want to be in on our conversation," she remarked.

"That won't be necessary," the officer responded.

Emily waved to Matt as she got into the van. "What's going on?" Matt asked, as he approached us.

"They want to speak with Emily about the car that almost ran over her," I informed him.

"Did you finally catch the guy?" Matt inquired.

"No, there was no report. Annie, who works in the chief's office, destroyed the records. It appears she's involved with Maggie's relatives," I explained.

"You found out who it was?" Matt questioned.

"Marc discovered it, and he should be here soon. He stayed over at Ash's place last night."

"This is getting interesting," Matt remarked, glancing at the officers. "Have any arrests been made? If Emily is harmed in any way, I'll personally see that she sues this entire town. What has happened will be all over the news. Can I have all four of your names? And why do four police officers need to question Emily?"

"I think it would be best if Emily came down to the police precinct to answer questions," the officer suggested.

"That's not going to happen. You have waited almost an entire year to ask her questions. You can wait another ten minutes," Matt firmly asserted.

Matt turned to me. "I'm going to grab a cup of coffee. Does anyone else want one?" He entered through Emily's back door and came out with a cup of coffee and a fresh donut, wearing a satisfied smile as he sat down.

"One of the perks of having a chef for your client is the fantastic food she makes," he said, taking another bite.

"Now, let's get down to business. Why has it taken you

almost a year to investigate what happened to Emily?" Matt asked.

"We only received the file this morning. It has been misplaced," the officer explained.

"Is that what you're calling it?" Matt questioned.

I spotted Emily and Kelsey returning to the driveway. They hurried to the back when I waved to her. "Darn, I was hoping you were gone. Okay, what do you want to know?" Emily asked.

"Tell us everything about the accident."

"It was no accident. Whoever drove that car tried to run me over. Lately, he's been following me and driving past my house. I didn't get a look at him because the windows were so dark. But the car is purple with white stripes. That's all I can tell you," Emily explained.

"Do you have any idea who would want to harm you? Do you have any enemies?" the officer inquired.

"Not to my knowledge," she replied.

Her frustration was evident. So I took over. "You know who it is. I've told you. If you can't do something about it, then we will." I knew Emily was staring at me. I refused to look at her. She would have to wait until these guys left.

"We have to have more evidence than your say so," one of the officers explained.

"Why?" I questioned.

"Do you really believe that we arrest everyone someone accuses of being guilty," the officer countered.

I watched Marc pull into the driveway with his son, Adam, and Ash Beckham. I shook their hands as they walked to where we stood, speaking to the police. "Marc, can you please tell these gentlemen how you discovered who was following Emily?"

"Sure, I asked Emily what the vehicle looked like and

who Maggie's family were, and then I checked out their place and saw the purple car there."

"Oh, Lordy. Do you think it's Maggie's family who wants to hurt me?" Emily asked.

"Who are you guys?" the officer asked again.

"Marc Breaux, Band of Navy Seals. I work with high intelligence and high security."

"I'm Ash Beckham. I work in the same field as Marc."

"My name is Kash Walker. I'm with the Army Rangers Special Ops. We rescue Americans that didn't make it out of certain countries, and we provide aid for innocent people," I explained.

"Yeah, what he said," Matt said. I was watching Emily and following her eyes. Judging by her expression, something was off, and she was about to find out. Emily was staring at Marc.

"I can't believe you! Emily said, looking at me. "You hired Marc to watch over me." She looked at Marc. "You told me Kash didn't hire you."

"I haven't taken a penny for being here. Adam and I have enjoyed being here for vacation. I did what I did because I consider you my friend," Marc clarified.

"You do?"

"Yes, I do."

"I'm sorry I said that." She looked at me. "I'm sorry, Kash."

"That's alright. Don't worry about it." She looked at the police, "Are you finished with your questioning?"

"Yes, if you happen to spot the car again, please call us," the officer replied, handing his card to Emily. I felt a surge of jealousy as I noticed how the officer looked at her. I wouldn't be surprised if he asked for her phone number. My thought was confirmed when he did just that.

"Why do you want to call me?" Emily inquired.

"I thought we could have dinner sometime," the officer suggested.

"No, I'm sorry. I don't have time for dinner with anyone. When I do have time to go out, it will be with Kash. But thank you for asking," Emily declined politely.

I smiled at the officer, and after they left, Emily turned to Marc, "Why would Maggie's family want to harm me?"

"It's not so much about wanting to harm you that concerns me. It's more about whether they want to eliminate you," Marc explained.

"Why?" Emily questioned.

"I suspect there might be an insurance policy out there, and they might be aware of it. Since you have the children, they may want to remove you from the equation," Marc elaborated.

"That's frightening," Emily admitted.

"I think you and the kids should stay with me," I blurted out, instantly regretting my words. Marc and Matt exchanged glances, and it was clear that I had misspoken. Ash said a bad word, and Emily regarded me as if I were crazy.

"Are you out of your mind? Why would you say that? I have to get busy and start cooking. I'll see you all later," Emily responded, picking up Kelsey and heading inside the house. I looked at the guys and smiled.

"I'll give her three more months, and then we'll be together. I need to keep her safe for now," I stated, determined to protect Emily and her family.

19

EMILY

DID I SAY THAT OUT LOUD? HOLY COW, KASH PROBABLY THINKS I'm too sure of myself to say that in front of his friends. What is wrong with me?

I couldn't get out of there fast enough. I was chuckling at myself as I got all the makings out for the wedding cake. This would be my eighth wedding cake in two months, and this one was going to be a carrot cake with vanilla buttercream frosting. I was going to do it in pieces. I had until Saturday, and I wanted this cake to be perfect for the upcoming wedding.

We were eating lunch when I heard the doorbell and went to answer it. There was a box on the porch. I saw the UPS truck driving away. I had no idea what it was. I hadn't ordered anything. I carried the box back to the kitchen to open it. "Hey there, sweet Kelsey, I wonder what we've got here." As I opened the box, I found something wrapped in a towel. However, I hesitated and decided to call Kash and inform him. Before I knew it, he and his friends had arrived, eager to investigate the mysterious delivery.

"What do you think it is? Who would have sent me something like this?" I asked, puzzled.

"I don't know. Why don't you wait inside until we take a look at it?" Kash suggested.

"Do you think it might be something bad?" I was watching Kash, and that's when I noticed his eyes had green in them. His lashes were so dark and long—lucky him.

"Emily, did you hear me?" Kash asked.

"I'm sorry. Yes, I'll go inside. Be careful. You don't know what's in there."

"Emily, we know what we are doing."

"Okay." I stepped back inside, but I could see through the screen door. Kash pulled the towel out of the box and unwrapped a pile of severed doll heads. Shocked, I opened the door and stepped back outside. "Why would anyone send me doll heads?" I stepped forward and looked more closely at them. "Oh my God, these are my dolls from when I was little. How did someone get my old dolls, and why did they tear their heads off? I remember leaving these at my dad's house. Who and how did they get my dolls?"

"Did you put them in a box that went to the thrift store?"

"No, my mom bought these for me. I would never have given them away. I wonder if Maggie gave them away. Do you think Maggie gave them away to her family? And that's who did this."

"I don't know. What the hell is this supposed to mean? It's absolutely bizarre," Kash said.

"I say whoever did this knew the dolls belonged to Emily and thought he would scare her," Matt said.

"Well, it doesn't scare me, but it makes me angry that someone did this to my dolls. I want to get rid of them. Let's throw them away," I said.

"I'll take them. You never know if we might need them.

We might have to use these to connect them with the car. The towel can be used for sure. It probably matches at least one other towel in their possession," Matt said.

As I looked at the men surrounding the box, it became apparent that they were experienced in handling such situations. Feeling somewhat out of my depth, I decided to let them handle the matter and returned to the kitchen to finish working on my cake. Kelsey had fallen asleep, so I carried her to her room, and Kash's dog, Max, followed us, making himself comfortable.

"EMILY, I'll take this box to my place for safekeeping. Yummy, something smells delicious. What are you cooking?" Kash asked.

"A wedding cake. Would you like some when it's done?"

How will you manage that? Won't they notice if you give them a wedding cake with a piece missing?"

I smiled and walked up to Kash. "Yes, but I always make sure I cook an extra pan just in case I need it. I'll bring you some when it's ready." I surprised myself when I got on my tiptoes and kissed him. He wrapped his arms around me, and I could feel his erection. "When is this going to happen?"

"When can you get a babysitter?" Kash whispered in my ear.

"Saturday, we can have dinner at your place. That way, I won't be far away."

"I'll cook dinner," Kash replied.

"I didn't know you could cook," I remarked, genuinely surprised.

"Who do you think cooks for me if I don't? Besides you, of course." Kash teased, chuckling. Then he drew me close and gazed into my eyes. "I've been waiting for almost a year for you, and I can't wait for Saturday night. I'll pick you up and walk you over to my place. Don't plan on going home until late."

"I can't wait either. Just you and me," I replied, and he kissed me again. In an impulsive moment, he pressed me against the wall, and my hands tangled in his hair. I had longed to feel his hair for a while. As he lifted me, I wrapped my legs around him, our clothes the only barrier between us. His calloused hands slipped inside my panties, and his fingers found their way between my heated folds. I couldn't help but make a sound as he inserted another finger,

stimulating my sensitive bud. I writhed in pleasure, attempting to stifle my cries but failing as he continued his intimate exploration. His lips claimed mine, swallowing the pleasure-filled sounds as he moved in and out of me. I was burning with desire for him, yearning to take him to my room and indulge in passionate lovemaking. Finally, I climaxed right there in his hand, and he cupped my throbbing core, his lips never leaving mine.

"THAT'S JUST a taste of what you will be getting Saturday night," Kash whispered as he lowered me back to the ground. The realization of his friends being outside the door suddenly dawned on me, and I glanced nervously toward it. Kash shook his head. "No one is there; they've already left," he assured me. He kissed me once more.

"Why don't you follow me to my room, and I can return the favor?" I suggested, unable to contain my desire.

"As much as I'd love to, sweetheart, I have a meeting downtown in ten minutes," Kash regretfully declined.

"It doesn't feel right that I climaxed and you didn't."

"You can make it up to me Saturday. Tell the babysitter to stay the night."

"Okay, I will." I looked at him with desire, and he returned the gaze, looking as though he wanted to devour me. I took a step closer, but then I remembered my cake. "Oh no, my cake!" I exclaimed, rushing to the oven. Luckily, it appeared perfect. I turned back to Kash with a smile

"I'll see you later."

"Okay, I'll see you later."

20

KASH

I couldn't get Emily off my mind as I walked into Angel's house. We were set to go into Kabul and rescue some trapped missionaries. They went against everyone's advice, and two of them were already dead because of it. Our friends had hidden them but couldn't hide them for much longer, so they needed to leave soon.

"Thursday morning, we depart for Kabul, Matt informed the team. All of us are going. We'll be gone for at least a week longer if complications arise. Kash, can you bring Max?"

I hesitated, not sure I wanted to take Max away from Emily. "No, I think I'll leave Max with Emily. I can borrow one of my friend's dogs. That way, I'll know Emily will at least have Max guarding them if anything happens. We'll reconvene at my house in two days."

As I headed home, all I could think of was how I would have to break our date for Saturday night. I pulled into my driveway, and at the same time, Emily pulled into her yard with the boys. It was Tuesday, so I knew she wouldn't be working tonight. I watched them all get out of the car and approached her as she stepped out.

"How about you all come to my house for a barbeque tonight? Hamburgers and hot dogs."

"We would love to have dinner with you. I'll bring a potato salad." She put Kelsey down, and I walked up to her. I have to cancel Saturday. We leave for Kabul on Thursday. When we get back, we'll most definitely have our night."

Emily surprised me when she went on her tiptoes and kissed me. "I'll be waiting anxiously." I grinned, bent my head, and kissed her again. It felt like this could be something I'd always yearn for.

EMILY WATCHED me as she ate her hamburger. "Tell me why you are going to Kabul. From what I know about what's happening there, the Taliban and ISIS have been lurking around. While you're there, maybe you can find out where Lara is. I'm worried because I haven't heard from her in a while. Lara has always sent me a message so I would know she's safe. I might be overreacting, but Lara has a tendency to intervene if she witnesses something wrong, especially if it involves a child."

"I'll ask around and see what I can find out, but we will be on the outskirts of Kabul. We are rescuing some missionaries. They might have heard something. I've been asking around about your brother."

"You have? Have you heard anything?" Emily asked a glimmer of hope in her eyes.

"I talked to a few of his buddies who were with him when he disappeared. All three of them said they didn't understand how he went missing. He was with them one moment, and the next, he was gone. Do you think he wanted to vanish?"

"I honestly don't know. I hadn't heard from Graham in six months before he went missing. Maggie said he came home for a visit, and he argued with our dad. Our father was different with his new family; he was demanding and controlling with Graham and me."

My mom had to make do with a fixed monthly allowance, which never changed whether we needed warm clothes or more food. At fifteen, I got my first job to help buy school clothes and support my mom, who worked ten hours a day. She ironed clothes to afford my hearing aids when I turned thirteen. Then she passed away, and we moved in with our father. It wasn't a pleasant experience."

"Your father seems to have changed for the better with his new family," I observed.

"I used to check on them when Jason was little, and our father had indeed transformed. He played with the kids, laughed with them, and Maggie wouldn't tolerate mistreatment. Perhaps he didn't love our mom; I'll never know."

"I'LL DO my best to locate Graham. Someone must have information," I assured her.

"Thank you, but maybe it's better if I leave it alone. What if he doesn't want to be found?"

"Do you want to know what I think? If he was a Marine, his disappearance could mean he's either dead or being held captive somewhere."

"That's what I've feared as well. That's why I pretended to be a journalist and went to Iran to find him. I'm sorry to burden you with my problems. That's not fair. First, we are neighbors with kids, and then I'm a nosey neighbor who won't let you have peace and quiet. Plus, I keep forcing food on you all the time."

"I never realized how much I enjoyed all of those things until your family moved in next door," I confessed, looking at Emily. Her smile tugged at my heartstrings. *No, this can't be happening. I want her, and she wants me—nothing else. I'm not going to deceive myself.*

"How about you join Kelsey and me for lunch tomorrow? Then I can put Kelsey to bed, and we won't have to wait until you return."

"What time should I come over?" I asked.

"Eleven-thirty; she takes an early nap."

I leaned across the table and kissed Emily passionately, savoring her lips as if I were making love to them. My heart raced, and I forgot to breathe. It felt as if I could climax right there, sitting outside as the kids played in the backyard.

"I have to give the little ones their bath for school. I'll see you tomorrow for lunch."

I couldn't help myself. I pulled Emily around the table and kissed her. "I'll see you tomorrow."

What have I done? I'm a nervous wreck. How can I get naked with Kash? He's used to being with tall, skinny models. I'm none of that. Oh, well, it is what it is. I'm not going to worry about my body anymore. Kash knows what he wants, and he wants me. That is all that matters for now.

21

EMILY

Lunch was ready when Kash showed up. I met him at the door. "I already fed Kelsey, and she's sleeping. Lunch is all ready for us."

He took my hand and bent his head, pulling my top over my head. "I'm not hungry for food. I'm hungry for you." My top landed on the table, and then he unbuttoned my pants. "Show me to your room." We walked past Kelsey's room, and Max growled. Kash chuckled as he followed behind me.

The minute we were next to the bed, he lowered me onto it and leaned over me. Are you sure you want to do this?" Kash asked me, and I stripped myself out of my pants. Kash took his tee shirt off, and then he stripped out of his jeans. He lay down beside me, looked into my eyes, and smiled. "Are you ready to have hot, sweaty sex with me?"

"I can't wait. I almost called you over last night."

"Damn, I almost came over here last night."

I giggled, and he took my bra off. My big boobs fit perfectly in his large hand, and his other hand pushed my panties off. Kash started kissing my neck, and then he took one of my breasts into his mouth. It felt so good. He moved to the next one, then down my body until his tongue touched my center, and I growled in pleasure. I was thrashing and bucking as his tongue worked its way to my nub. Right before I orgasmed, he raised and slid his large hard erection inside me. I thought I had died and gone to heaven. We pleasured each other for two hours before I heard Kelsey talking to Max.

"Come back tonight. We've just got started." He kissed me long and hard before he got up and dressed. "Can you sit with Kelsey while I take a quick shower?"

"Yes."

"Thank you." The shower was only ten minutes, and then I walked outside, where Kash played with Kelsey. "Hey, sweetie." I knew my face was red, and I tried not to look Kash in the eyes. He put his arms around me and kissed me.

"I'll see you tonight. We are going to make love all night long. I leave tomorrow."

"I'll see you tonight," I said, looking up at him. He bent his head and kissed me again. I watched him walk away. I picked Kelsey up and walked back inside the house. I had a massive grin on my face. I started laundry and read to Kelsey while the clothes were washing. The afternoon went by fast. I picked the boys up from school. I didn't like them walking since I got those doll heads in the mail. Whoever sent them had a sick mind, and I didn't want them near someone like that.

"Emily, can we get me a laptop if I start doing more work? I have so much homework that I have to do on the internet. I've been waiting to do my homework until I get to school."

"Jason, you should have told me you needed a laptop. I should have known you needed one. I'm sorry. You don't have to work more; you work hard enough as it is. I have a laptop you can use until tomorrow after school. We'll get you a new laptop for yourself."

"I didn't know you had a laptop."

"I keep all of my recipes on it. I haven't used it since I moved here. I also have a printer. Let's get them now. They're in the garage."

"That's great. Thanks. Are you and Kash dating?"

I felt my face burning. "We aren't dating but seeing if we want to. Does that bother you?"

"Heck no, it doesn't bother me. I like Kash. He's cool."

"Okay, but I'm not saying we are together. We are just seeing if we want to be together for now. Do you know what I mean?"

"Yes, I'm fifteen years old. I know about boys and girls."

I chuckled and ruffled Jason's hair. "We need to start checking out driver education for you."

"Really, Emily, that would be so cool. Thank you. When can we do that?"

"I'll call around to a few places next week. How does that sound?" I remembered how badly I wanted to check driver education out. I felt bad that I hadn't talked to him about it before.

"That sounds great. Thank you so much. Can we afford it?"

"Yes, we can afford it. Let me worry about the money, and you take care of being a teenager. I'll pick you up a driver's handbook to study when I'm in town today."

"Okay, that sounds great. I have a few friends that say you really have to study it. I can't wait."

Jason was doing homework, the younger kids were in bed, and I was a nervous wreck. I knew Kash would be here in two hours, so I got a pen and paper and wrote up some dinner menus for next week's meals. I also wrote down some of the driver-ed schools to call next week. I saw the lights go off in Jason's room. I felt like a teenager sneaking around at night with my boyfriend. The house was quiet, and I stepped outside to see if Kash was there. I saw him walking up from the beach.

When he reached me, he smiled. "Why don't we sit out here for a little bit and talk? I don't want you to think I'm taking advantage of you."

"I'm thirty-two. I know if someone is taking advantage of me. I don't want you to think I'm taking advantage of you." I smiled, and Kash chuckled. "Kash, it's not like we are going to do this every night, right? I don't know about you, but I've been waiting anxiously for this. We will enjoy each other all night or most of the night." He pulled me into his arms.

"That's what I was hoping you would say," he said, kissing my neck.

We walked into the house and went straight to my room. Kash had my clothes off before we fell onto the bed. I giggled as he spread my legs. He grinned when I inhaled. My breathing was erratic, just knowing what he meant to do. I put the pillow over my head so the children couldn't hear me. Kash was driving me wild. I reached down and pulled his shirt off. "Take your pants off. I want to feel you."

"Are you sure about this?"

"I pulled him down to me and kissed him as my shaking hands ran down his back. "This is all I want," I whispered with a light breath that fanned across his ear. We made love for hours before both of us were exhausted and fell asleep.

I woke up to Kash kissing my neck. "Wake up, sweetheart," he whispered in my ear. Before I could respond, he pulled me down on top of him. He wrapped his arms around me and rolled me onto my back. His knee nudged my legs apart, and he stretched out between my thighs, bracing himself on his elbows as he looked down at my flushed face.

My heart raced. I went utterly still and waited to see what he would do. "*Don't let go,*" I whispered to myself.

"I won't, sweetheart."

I stopped thinking when I realized that I had said that out loud. Kash gently lowered himself to me. His hard chest rubbed against my breast as he leaned over her to put on a condom. I couldn't believe I hadn't thought about that. Shivers cascaded down my arms and legs when he began to nuzzle the side of my neck. His breath was sweet and warm against my skin, and when he tugged on my earlobe, I felt a jolt of longing all the way down to my toes.

"This isn't a bad idea," I whispered, tilting my head to give him better access. I kissed him and knew I was getting in over my head. *I will not fall in love,* I repeated in my mind over and over.

Kash raised his head up. "Want me to stop?"

"No." I reached up and kissed his chin. "No, I want you to kiss me."

Kash was suddenly eager and hot, as though it was his first time. He knew how to please a woman. God knows he'd perfected his technique over the years, but this was different. He continued to make hot, sweet love to me.

I was losing control. Kash was obviously losing control as well. It was like I was going to explode.

"Kash." I didn't know if I shouted his name or sighed it. His hands had moved between my thighs, and he was driving me out of my mind. He knew just where to touch and exactly how much pressure to exert. I writhed in his arms, pleading with him to come to me.

Again, I was desperate to feel every inch of him to wrap myself in his warmth. His breathing became more labored, and that excited me even more. I would die if he continued to torment me.

Kash delayed as long as he could to give me as much pleasure as I was giving him. My response made it impossible to wait any longer. His mouth covered mine, and he moved between my thighs and slowly sank into my liquid heat. I was so tight, so hot, he groaned from the sheer bliss. He stayed completely still inside me, panting as he whispered my name.

When he came inside me, I cried out. The ecstasy was overwhelming. He rolled to his side and pulled me with him. Kash held me and stroked me, his touch tender now. Neither of us spoke, both content for the moment. The minutes ticked by, and I fell asleep in his arms.

In the middle of the night, I awoke. He was still there. I was surprised and content. I closed my eyes and went back to sleep. I woke up when Kash held me and stroked me, his touch tender. I closed my eyes. When I opened my eyes again, he was gone. I looked at the clock and knew he had already left for overseas. I pulled myself out of bed, then grabbed Kash's pillow and smelled it. It smelt just like him. *I won't ever wash this pillowcase.* I took a quick shower before waking the kids.

22

KASH

I SAT BACK IN THE PLANE WITH MY EYES CLOSED. I WASN'T sleepy; I just didn't want to talk. I wanted to be quiet and remember every minute I spent with Emily. I had never wanted to stay with someone more than I wanted to stay with her and those kids. I wondered if she felt what I felt.

"Are you going to sleep the entire trip?" Angel said, sitting down next to me. "Or did you have an all-nighter with another long-legged blonde?"

I opened one eye. "Do you mind? I'm resting; stop bothering me."

"Oh my God, who is she?"

"I don't know what you are talking about." I kept my eyes closed, hoping he would leave.

"No, it's not one of your bimbos. It's Emily. You got it bad for Emily."

"Shut up," I growled, showing my teeth. "You will not say one word about Emily."

"I can't believe you. What about all of those kids? How will you have any kind of sex life with ten kids?"

"There are five kids."

"Now, there are five. But you'll be popping your own kids out as well."

"I didn't say I was going to get married. I'm finished talking about Emily."

"Well, hell," Angel said as he returned to his seat. I could feel his eyes boring into the back of my seat. I took a deep breath. No one was going to mess up my memories. Emily looked so sweet lying there, her hair spread across my chest. I almost woke her for one more tumble, but I knew she had a full day ahead of her.

We landed on a private landing strip out of Kabul, far enough away that the Taliban wouldn't detect us. We were supposed to meet up with someone who knew where the missionaries were. We waited a day and a half before anyone showed up, and when he did, he was bleeding from a gunshot wound. It wasn't life-threatening. Angel had it patched up in no time. I saw Matt standing there and knew he wanted to ask something. I decided to ask instead so Matt wouldn't feel embarrassed over questions about Lara West.

"Have you seen or heard anything about a white woman who is undercover? She's a reporter."

"Are you talking about Lara West?"

"Yes."

"She's in hiding. One of the big-shot ISIS men wanted her for himself. He remembered her from before. When he captured her, he beat her, and Lara fought back. She grabbed hold of his knife and stabbed him. She thought he was dead, but unfortunately for her, he lived. Lara has the entire country hunting for her. I wish I knew where she was. I'd tell her so she could get the hell out of here. Her cameraman will be coming with us."

"Damn, her. Can't she stay out of trouble for one year out of her life? I swear she makes me so angry," Matt growled. We looked at Matt, and then he walked away. I knew he was upset and scared for Lara. He didn't want to be because the woman he loved broke his heart and never told him why. I walked behind him. "I'm sure she's alright."

"I hope the hell she is. But what about the next time? Damn her. I don't know what happened, but she has been trying to kill herself since she broke up with me. Maybe Emily can say something to her if she manages to get herself out of here alive."

I didn't know what to say, so I kept quiet. "Let's go talk to this guy and find out what is going on with the missionaries."

When we got back, Angel looked ready to kill someone, and even easy-going Ryan Grant's face was red like he was going to blow a fuse. "What's going on?"

"They don't have a way for the missionaries to get to the plane."

I scratched my head. Then I ran a hand over my face. We'd already wasted three days. I'd been gone a week already. It could take us forever to get these ladies. But we had to get them. We were paid a lot of money to bring these people home. "Then how are we supposed to rescue them?"

"You'll have to get them. I tried, and I didn't get anywhere near where they were hiding, and some crazy bastard shot me."

"You'll have to take us. We don't know where they are."

"No, Kash. We can't risk it. The job was to pick them up here and get them out. It's too dangerous."

I ignored Angel. "What kind of vehicles do we have."

"We have a bus. I can take you to it and show you where they are hiding." The man replied, relieved this was getting finished.

"Let's get this done." Ryan, Angel, and I drove with

Hamil to get the bus. It took three hours. The sun would be going down soon. We needed to hurry, but we couldn't bring any attention to ourselves. We were about an hour from the hiding place when a vehicle quickly came up behind us. I thought for sure we were dead, but it went around us.

The sun had gone over the horizon when we pulled into a long driveway. It was pitch black, and we didn't turn our lights on. They had a curfew here and meant it when they said no one was out after dark. We would have to wait until morning before we left. We parked behind the building and went through a back door. No one was around. We walked to the back of the building, and Hamil knocked three times, then another three times before the door opened. Women in the full dress were standing in a huddle. When they saw Hamil, they ran to us. All of them started talking at once. Hamil raised his hand. "One at a time."

"Thank the Lord; you are here. We have to leave tonight. We got a message from Lara. She said they are looking for us and will not stop until they kill all of us."

I looked at the woman. "Where is Lara? Is she badly injured?"

"We don't know where she is, but we need to leave. We'll have to drive in the dark."

I looked over at Ryan, and he shrugged his shoulders. "This is what we are going to do. We'll take turns driving while one of us runs in front of the bus with this small flashlight. We'll need all of our concentration to see, so we need everyone to be quiet."

I knew Angel wouldn't like this, but we had to do what we had to do. "I'll run the first ten miles, and then you can choose between you who runs the next."

Just as I thought, Angel shook his head before I finished

talking. "What if they sneak up on us? The first person to die will be the runner. I don't like this at all."

"Do you have a better idea?"

"I know what I'll say if anyone asks me to accompany you again. I'll say hell no and stay on my island."

"I'll remember that next time." I looked at the woman who did all the talking. "Where did you get the bus?"

"We got it from one of our supporters. He has since been executed for helping to get milk and food for the starving children."

"The person who killed him, is it the same person who Lara injured?"

"Yes, the same person. So, you can see how dangerous it is for her to stay here."

The woman looked at me. "Lara won't listen to anyone. She said she's staying until she can notify the world about the starving children."

"I hope she stays alive to tell her story." We left thirty minutes later. I took my time running my ten miles. We all knew to pace ourselves when running, especially as far as we had to go. I still had plenty of energy when Ryan took over. I climbed on top of the bus to see if anyone was after us. I didn't see any headlights anywhere. I stayed up there to keep my eyes on the back of us. I heard a noise and saw Angel pulling himself up over the rack on top of the bus.

"What are we going to do when the sun comes up?"

"We'll just keep on going. We knew this would not be a piece of cake when we decided to save these people. We do what we need to do to stay alive. I hope we don't have to worry about getting into a gunfight with anyone. I'm sure their guns are much bigger than ours."

"Why don't you get some sleep? I'll keep my eyes open."

"I'll just lay down here. At least I can't roll off with these racks here." I slept for about an hour when Angel tapped my shoulder. "What is it?"

"I see headlights. They're a long way behind us, but I'm sure they're moving a hell of a lot faster than us. We need to get Ryan off that road and get the fuck out of here."

"Fuck." We flew over the bus and ran to where Ryan was. The bus stopped, and I could hear the ladies getting anxious. I looked at Angel, "I'm going to get on the front of the bus and hang on. While you drive, I'll shine the flashlight on the road. Don't worry that I'll fall; I won't. Let's go." Angel shook his head as he entered the bus.

"If you ladies want to help, you will shut up, so we can do our job." Angel was never one to mix words. I had doubts about us making it to the plane on time, but I kept them to myself.

I walked to the front of the bus with my flashlight. When I turned my head, Ryan had joined me with his flashlight. "Are you sure you want to do this?"

"I'm sure." We hung on for our lives. Angel was one of the best drivers I knew, so I knew if anyone could get us the hell out of here, it was him. He drove like a madman. I felt like I was on a crazy whipping ride. I looked over at Ryan, and he had a massive grin on his face. I laughed out loud. The idiot was having fun. When dawn was breaking, we climbed into the bus. When a bullet shattered the back window, I knew we had to kill the driver.

I looked at Ryan. "Save your bullets for the driver. He's the only one we have to kill. The plane isn't far. If we get him, we have it made." Ryan nodded and aimed. He shot him on the first shot.

"How often did you say you went hunting with your dad?"

"Too many to count."

We saw the plane. It was taxing its way toward us. "I want you ladies to run into the plane. Don't stop to talk, don't stop for anything. Just run like the devil is after you because he is." As soon as the bus stopped rolling, everyone started running. The plane was in the air, and the jeep was driving down the airway, shooting at us. Matt shouted, and I ran up to the cockpit.

"Did you see her?"

"No, but she's the one who sent a message that we needed to leave while it was dark. At least we know she's alive." He nodded his head and didn't say another word.

We ended up in another country because one of the women was ill and needed to go to a hospital. We were there four days before they allowed us to leave. We ended up in Germany for another three days. Then we headed home. I was anxious to see Emily, and I wondered if she regretted us being together. I didn't regret any of it. I couldn't wait to hold her in my arms. I knew I was falling hard for Emily, kids and all. I wanted all of them in my life. I didn't know if it was forever, but I wanted to find out if she felt the same way I did. Right now, it felt like forever to me.

"Do you mind if I crash at your place tonight?" Matt asked.

"Yeah, me too," Ryan said.

"I might as well stay there too," Angel said.

There went me sneaking into bed with Emily. I looked at my watch; it was two in the morning.

23

EMILY

I was excited because Kash called and said he would see me in the morning. I went to sleep around eleven. Jason was still awake, and since it wasn't a school night, I didn't tell him what time to go to bed. I never had to say anything to Jason. He knew what to do.

A slight noise woke me up. I left my room and went into the living room, where I saw two men fighting with Jason. One of them had their hand over his mouth to keep him quiet. I shouted for the boys to get Kelsey and go over to Kash's house. Brian ran into the room. "Get Kelsey right now and go to Kash's. Get your brothers and run!" I screamed at the men, picked up something—I didn't know what—and ran to where they were hurting my brother.

I hit one of them with the object in my hand, which turned out to be a vase. He turned and slugged me in the face, but I didn't let it knock me out. I would risk my life for my brother. *Max, where are you? I screamed.* I could hear him. That's when I realized he was locked in Kelsey's room. I heard glass shatter, and Max came through the front door. He headed for the man who had a hold of Jason. Out of the corner of my eye, I saw Jason roll onto the floor. I could barely stand. It took all I had not to fall over. The man wouldn't stop beating me. Then he grabbed me and ran out the door. I fought as much as I could. I knew Max wouldn't allow that other man to hurt the kids. One more slug under my chin with his fist, and I blacked out.

I SAW Emily's front door open when we pulled into my driveway. My heart fell into the pit of my stomach. Something was wrong. I jumped from my vehicle and heard a loud growl. I turned around and saw Max growling at Angel and the others. He had blood all over him. "Max, stay." He sat down, and Angel beat me in the house. Jason was lying on the floor, and blood was everywhere. A dead man was lying next to Jason. We could tell Max had killed him. His neck was ripped open.

Angel ran to Jason. "He's alive!" he shouted over the noise of the other kids crying. They were in the corner of the room. I called my mom and told her we needed her and that I didn't have time to explain.

I ran into every room, hunting for Emily. *Where the hell is she?* I went into the room where the kids were and picked Kelsey up. The others wrapped their arms around me. I looked at them and could tell they weren't involved in the fighting. Kelsey's bedroom window was shattered when I walked up to it. I could see dog hair caught in pieces of the glass. Max must have been locked in this room and busted his way out. I talked to Emily at ten, so these guys must have gotten here between ten and two by the looks of the dead man.

"Do any of you know where Emily is?"

"I do. That other man took her. He beat her up badly. But she hit him over the head with a vase. When he put her in the truck, she kicked him, and he slugged her, and she fell over. Emily told us to run to your house, but I couldn't get them to follow me. So, we locked the door in Kelsey's room and got in the closet. Max jumped through the window to help Jason and Emily. I forgot to let him out. Is Jason dead?"

"No. Angel is with him. Grammy Marge is coming. She'll take you to my house and care for you while I find Emily. Did you say the man that took her was in a truck?"

"Yeah, the man had a truck. I don't know if Emily has her hearing aids. Maybe she can't hear anything," he cried. Thank God my mom showed up at that moment.

"What happened here?" my mom whispered, wiping tears from her eyes. "Where is Emily?"

"Mom, we don't know where she is. We just got back from Kabul fifteen minutes ago. Now I have to find Emily. Would you please take the kids to my house?"

"Of course I will." She reached for Kelsey, who wouldn't let go of me.

"Kelsey, sweetheart, go with Grammy Marge."

Brian told my mom everything as I tried to untangle Kelsey. Finally, she went to my mom.

Ryan walked up to me. I knew he had found something. We wanted to get all of our information together before the police got there. "This guy is Jasper Cook. He's been in and out of prison for all sorts of things, and he's also been known to be hired out as a hitman. He's never been charged with it, so for a small amount of money, the bastard will kill anyone."

"Fuck, fuck, and fuck." My fist went through the wall. I shouted so loud I could kill that bastard if he wasn't already dead. "How is Jason?"

"He was stabbed a couple of times. Angel said he would be okay. He's starting to come around. I thought you would like to know."

I walked over to where Jason lay on the sofa. "Hey buddy, I want you to know you are a hero. You saved your brothers and sister. They are over at my place with my mom. You have to go to the hospital for a couple of days. I will take care of everything."

"Did they kill Emily?"

"No. I'm going to be honest with you. Max killed one of the men, and the other one took Emily. I'm going to find her. That I will promise you, I'll find her. Angel is going to follow you to the hospital. If anyone there asks you who your guardian is, you tell them I am. Angel will fill out all of the paperwork for you. I'll talk to you later today if I have time. Now, the ambulance is going to take you to the hospital. I'm sorry I can't go with you."

"I want you to find Emily."

I bent down and hugged him. I hated leaving him. I kissed his forehead. Then Matt, Ryan and I made our way to Maggie's relatives.

I hoped that I had a chance to kill one of her relatives. I knew they were responsible for this.

I HAD horrendous pain in my head when I moved, and I vomited all over myself. I lay there trying to remember what had happened. That's when my eyes flew open. That man had taken me from my home. Jason, oh Jason. I remember seeing him roll from that fucker when Max charged the guy and went straight for his neck.

I knew Max killed him quickly. I heard the gurgling

coming from him as Max bit down on his neck. I was glad he was dead. I wish Max would have gotten both of them. The one that took me knew he was next. That's why he took me with him.

I had to get out of here. *Where am I?* It felt damp and cold. I was freezing, but I didn't care. *I believe I'm in a cave or something in the mountains.* I knew there were all kinds of caves in these mountains. It was so dark.

My hands were tied together behind me. When I tried standing, my head hit the top. I can't even think. I have to have a plan. I sat down and tried getting my hands under me. I needed my hands in front of me. I had to get this rope off. I was too scared to cry. I wanted out of here. That was the only thought I had in my head. I walked on my knees until I fell on my face. That just added to my pain.

I screamed as loud as I could before I shook myself. Stop Emily, you're psyching yourself out, shut the hell up, and find a way out of here.

I rolled to my side and tried to get my arms in front of me. I had pulled my right shoulder. I heard a pop, but I didn't care. *Work through the pain.* I had my hands in front of me. Now, I could get out of there. It hurt so much when I tried straightening my arms that I had to stop.

I brought my hands to my mouth and started hunting for the spot where the rope was tied. I knew the tears were falling, but I wouldn't let my emotions take over. Jason needed me right now, and I had to escape this place. I'm sure the boys called the cops. They must be frantic hunting for me. I stopped, and a sob left my lips. Kash will be home by now.

He'll know what to do. He'll take care of the children. Finally, I got the rope off. I crawled until I saw some light. There was a boulder in front of the entrance. He must have thought I would die back here. Hopefully, that is what he thought, and I can get out of here before he returns. It was dark when I finally got the boulder out of my way, enough to squeeze through.

I stood up. That's when I looked down at my foot. It was swollen and purple. I couldn't step down. *What am I going to do?* I limped along until I found a stick. It helped me move a little faster. I decided I should move off this path where I was in the opening. I needed to stay hidden.

I FELT like I was going to be sick. I kept going. I was moving so slowly. I had to stop. I took deep breaths. My legs were shaky. I bent over and started vomiting. I didn't think I would ever stop. He kicked me so many times he must have ruptured something inside of me. Hell, I don't know anything about sickness or why I'm throwing up. I need to learn this stuff, I have children now.

I stopped again. I was crying now. If I die, those monsters will take the children. There must be an insurance policy. That would be the only reason why they want the kids. I stepped down, and my foot landed in a hole. I lost my balance and tumbled down the side of the mountain. I couldn't have saved myself if I had wanted to. When I stopped, I shut my eyes and went to sleep.

24

KASH

I DIDN'T BOTHER KNOCKING. I RIPPED THE TRAILER DOOR OPEN. The bastard was sitting in a chair with a beer in his hand, watching sports on the television. He jumped up and started shouting. I pushed him back down. I had to force myself not to kill him. The fucker hired someone to kill Emily.

"I will give you to the count of five to tell me where Emily is," I snarled. I started counting.

"I don't know what you are talking about!" he shouted.

I kept counting. "Stop counting. Who are you guys?"

I picked him up and slammed my fist in his face three times. "One of the men you hired talked to us before he was killed. He told us you hired him and another guy to kill Emily. Now, I will ask you again. Where the fuck is Emily?"

"I don't know where she is. I didn't have anything to do with any of this. The guy lied to you. Get out of my house. I'm calling the cops!"

"They are already on their way. You see, Emily told them about the purple car following her."

"What's that noise?"

"Oh, it's my buddy busting your car up."

"Stop," he tried pushing past me. I took that to mean he wanted to fight.

"Did you see that, Ryan? He wants to fight."

"No, I don't. I want all of you to leave." That's all I let him say before I started beating him until Ryan pulled me off of him.

"Give him time to talk. If I were you, I would spill the beans before my buddy here kills you."

"Look, I had nothing to do with this. My brother hired those men. I didn't know anything about it until that guy showed up."

"Where is she?" I shouted in his face.

"The guy said he dumped her body in a cave about twenty miles from here. I told him he needed to see if she was alive. He left about ten minutes ago."

I screamed so loud, then I picked the guy up and threw him through the window.

"Stop!" Ryan shouted. "We have to have him show us the way."

I could barely breathe. We went out as Matt picked the guy up. "Put him in the truck. He will show us where Emily is, or I will kill his ass right now. He can ride in the back with me."

The man directed us into the mountains. "Step on it. We might catch the fucker," I told Ryan. They wouldn't let me drive; I was shaking too much. I prayed all the way we would find Emily alive. I knew I was going to kill the other one. He was the one who hurt Emily. I let out a roar again, thinking about him hurting her. I refused to think about him killing her.

"Damn it, Kash, you almost made me wreck. Stop roaring in my ear!"

"I couldn't help it. It just came out. I'm sorry." I let my fist fly right into the guy's jaw.

"Don't knock him out. We'll never find Emily," Ryan said as he stepped on the gas.

"We'll find her because this guy knows exactly where the cave is. Don't you?" He didn't answer me. I slugged the bastard again. I could see Ryan and Matt shaking their heads.

"Pull over," Matt told Ryan. Ryan pulled over, and Matt got out. "Kash, change places with me."

"You're taking up fucking time."

"Then change."

"Fuck." I got out and changed places, and Ryan stepped on the gas.

"It's not much further up here. There's his truck."

I jumped out and walked to the guy's door when Matt beat me to it. We pushed him ahead of us. We started walking when I heard someone shouting, "You bitch, I'm going to kill you. You should be dead already."

I ran as fast as I could. I had to reach Emily before he killed her. Ryan was right behind me. I couldn't see anyone at first, then I saw a man crawling out of a hole in the mountain. As he stood up, I let him have it. I was battering him until Ryan pulled me away.

"Where is she?" The sun was coming up by now. I could see the fear on his face. "What's the matter? Are you afraid to fight a man?" I growled in his face. "Can you only fight women who are small and defenseless?" I hit him again. "Answer me, you bastard."

"I don't know where she is. She moved the boulder and got out. She must be dead somewhere. She was..."

He didn't get a chance to say anything else. Ryan grabbed him and started beating the crap out of him while I ran around trying to find Emily. I looked on the ground for tracks. I just couldn't stop thinking about her lying somewhere dead.

I looked over at Matt. I knew he had something to tell me. "Just say it."

"He said he slammed her foot with the truck door, so she won't be able to walk far."

I couldn't talk; I felt the tears brimming in my eyes. I should have stayed with her. I should have gone after Maggie's family and not have left it to the police. I didn't know if they even interviewed them. I kept on walking, shouting her name.

I FELT like I had been out of it for days, but I knew it couldn't be that long. I was so thirsty that I could barely swallow. Everything hurt. I touched the top of my head and found out my hair was matted with dried blood. I looked down when I felt stings.

I had ants all over me. I tried standing. It took a while, but I managed. I started brushing ants off, and everything returned to me. I let out a sob. I had to make sure I saved myself. I had my children to think of. I would survive for them. I would not let anyone find me; I had to hurry. I took a step on the injured foot and fell. I let out another sob. *Emily, stop it. If you start to feel sorry for yourself, you will end up dead.*

I thought I heard someone behind me, and I hobbled away as fast as I could. I knew I was crying, but I couldn't help it. I saw the ground at my feet move, and I panicked. I jumped sideways and fell further down the mountainside. I caught hold of a root sticking up.

I could hear water running. I had to reach that water. Where was the sound coming from? I just knew in my mind if I could find that water, I would be completely healed. I know that sounds crazy. But my mind wasn't working as it should. I had to find that water. I couldn't remember when I last drank water. *How long have I been away from home?*

I lay on the mountain floor and started praying. "God, please help me get home. Help Kash find me before I die. Those kids need me. I love them so much. I need them. Dear Lord, please watch over me. Please don't let any snakes come around me."

I kept talking as I pulled myself up off the ground. My hair hung forward on my face; I kept pushing it out of my eyes. I could hear the sound of a brook. I started hurrying to get that drink of water, which was my other mistake. I fell and rolled until I landed in the water. It wasn't a little brook. It was a vast river. When I went under, I was able to make it back to the top, and I looked around for something to grab hold of. I saw a tree branch. I wasn't worried because I was a good swimmer, but my shoulder was killing me.

I reached out for the limb with my other arm and grabbed it. I held on with all the strength I had. It seemed like I hung on forever in that ice-cold water before something slammed into my side, and I lost hold of the limb.

I saw something pink down the side of the mountain. I half ran, and half slid my way down to it. I went to pick it up and saw the blood on the leaves. I held a piece of cloth that was caught on a twig. I looked at it and knew it was a piece of Emily's pajamas. I'd seen her in them before.

"What do you have there?" Ryan asked as he and Matt slid down the side of the mountain. I looked up and saw Angel. "How's Jason? How did you get here?"

"I came with the police. Jason is going to be okay. I'm sure he'll be having nightmares for a while. He is so very lucky; he had two knife wounds, and both of them were close to his organs. He's a great kid. He wanted me to help find Emily. What's that?"

"It's a piece of Emily's pajamas. See the blood. She was here. Emily! Emily!" I shouted as loud as I could. I prayed she could hear us.

"What's that?" Ryan asked. We all slid further down the mountain. "She was here. She has to be nearby. By the looks of it, she might have fallen down the mountain." Ryan shook his head. "I think we need to shout her name and get the hell down there. I can hear the river."

We all ran down, shouting Emily's name. We came to the river and saw where she slid in. "Fuck!" I shouted. "Why is this happening to Emily? Emily!" I screamed at the top of my lungs. I looked around at the area. "She's a good swimmer. I've seen her in the ocean. She can swim as well as I can. She might be on the bank somewhere." I took off running. The water was freezing. I couldn't imagine how cold she must be.

I refused to think about her not being alive. She would never allow herself to die. She knew the kids needed her. I needed her. "Emily, we're here, sweetheart. It's us. If you can hear me, say something." We walked for another forty-five minutes when we saw where she climbed out of the water. The mud showed where her fingers clawed at it to grab hold to save her life. "Emily, sweetheart, can you hear me?"

"There she is," Angel said, running.

"Emily." We all reached her together. She had pulled herself out of the water and was lying on her stomach. I fell to my knees. I touched her, and she started fighting. She didn't know who we were. I gently touched her face, and she turned her head and opened her eyes. Then she closed them again. She was freezing. I looked over at Angel. "She's freezing."

"Let's get her out of those clothes."

"Here, she can have my shirt."

"Mine too."

I had two shirts tossed at me while Angel checked her for injuries, cursing the entire time. We took her torn, wet top off, and I gasped when I saw her poor body. I swore right there that man was going to die. "I don't know how she survived."

"Emily, sweetheart, can you hear me?"

"She doesn't have her hearing aids in."

I touched her face again, and she opened her eyes. "Can you keep your eyes open?"

"No."

"Why not?"

"Because your handsome friend is looking at my body."

Angel chuckled. "He's a doctor."

"I know; I lost my hearing aids." The tears started to fall. She looked at Angel. "How is Jason?"

"He's going to be okay," Angel answered. "Can you tell me where you hurt?"

"I think my foot is broken, and I have some busted ribs. My head hurts. I think I might have a concussion and need stitches where he hit me with a crowbar. My shoulder is pulled out of its socket. And I think every inch of my body is bruised. I'm sorry, guys, but I won't be able to walk out of here, and I keep blacking out."

"I'll carry you out of here, don't worry about that," I said. I was still talking to her when she blacked out. "Why do you think she's blacking out?"

"She needs to be in the hospital right now. There is more

wrong than what she said. Look at her side. I found it when we put the dry shirt on her, but I didn't want to say anything to scare her."

I looked at her side and almost lost it. There was a piece of a tree limb piercing her side. I don't know how far it went in, but it was as thick as a pencil. "How are we going to carry her? It seems like it would be dangerous even to move her."

Angel got on the phone and called an ambulance, only to be told one was already there. When I turned my head, the police chief was walking to where we were. Ryan explained everything to him. I looked up at Matt, and he was watching Emily.

"She's awake again."

Emily opened her eyes in a panic. I calmed her. "Emily, I'm going to carry you out of here. The ambulance is waiting for you." I bent to pick her up, and she screamed before blacking out. "Call and let the ambulance know we are on our way. They need everything ready when we get there."

25

EMILY

I LAY THERE WITH MY EYES SHUT, AND THEN MY EYES FLEW open. Kash looked at me and smiled. "Where are the kids? Where is Jason?"

"He's in another room. He will be discharged tomorrow, and the kids are with my mom."

"What happened? Who were those men?"

"Maggie's relatives hired them. They are both dead. But the one who had you said they were hired to kill the entire family. But Max jumped through Kelsey's window and stopped them."

"Please remind me to buy him a steak. Why did they want us dead?"

"Because there was an insurance policy, there were actually two of them. Your dad and Maggie both had one. Her cousin confessed that the lawyer and the cousins were in on it together. They would split the money; all they had to do was eliminate all of you."

"If Max hadn't been there, we would have all been murdered." Tears fell from her eyes. "The kids must be so scared. Tell me the truth, how is Jason doing?"

"I'm doing okay. Don't worry about me. I want you to get well." He broke down and almost fell on top of me, crying.

"I'm going to get well quickly, I promise. Now sit down so I can look at you."

"You look horrible," Jason said, looking at me. Kash chuckled. I looked at him and shook my head. "That man hurt you really bad."

"He beat me up. But I fell down a mountain and landed in the river where something hit my side. I can remember swimming with all my strength to reach the bank." I looked at Kash, "Then Kash found me, and my hero rescued me."

"There were four of us who found you?"

"I know. I'm trying not to remember all of them seeing me without my top on and my pajama bottom slit up to my waist. The only thing holding it together was the elastic band." I felt my eyes closing. Kash had hold of my hand. He brought it to his lips and kissed each of my fingers. I looked at him. "I lost my hearing aids," I said as my eyes shut.

Jason smiled. "She is always losing her hearing aids or giving them away."

"I have another pair for her. Jason, tell me what you remember about Graham?"

"He was the best brother. When he visited, he always played games with us. Graham and Emily loved us. They would always tell us they did. That's because their mother always told them she loved them. My mom was the same way. My dad never told us he loved us. But I knew he did. Mom said it was just the way he was brought up.

"I miss my big brother. I don't know if he's still alive. I hope he is. I remember Emily had a huge argument with my father because he wouldn't help her find him. When she went to Iran as a reporter, it scared my dad. He turned her in because he was afraid she would get killed over there.

Maybe one day Graham will show up. Wouldn't that be great?"

"Yeah, it would be. Come on; I'll walk you back to your room."

WHEN I WOKE UP AGAIN, I was alone. At first, I was frightened, and then I remembered I was in the hospital. I decided to get a gun to keep in my room. I would keep it in the safe. I would know where it was if I needed it. I would never take a chance like that again. Those bastards could have murdered all of us if Max hadn't been there. My entire body hurt. I hit the button for the nurse.

"Hi Emily, how can I help you? Are you in a lot of pain? I can give you something for the pain if you need it."

"I don't want any pain medicine. Can I get up and take a shower? I feel so dirty. How many days have I been here?"

"You've been here three days. I'll call the doctor and see what he says." Angel and Kash walked into the room. "Here he is right now."

"You're my doctor?"

"Yes, does that bother you?"

"No, I know you're a great doctor. Can I shower?"

"Let's wait until tomorrow. I want to look at your side where a piece of a limb pierced you. It went deep."

"That's what it was. I was holding on to a branch in the river when something hit my side and knocked me off. It was another tree. Thankfully, I could reach the bank before I blacked out." I looked at both of them. "How did that bastard die? The one who put me in the cave?"

I watched Kash explain what had happened. "There was

a lookout, and he jumped off of it. I tried grabbing him, but he was too quick for me."

"Good. I wonder how many family members Maggie has."

"Just the cousins. One died, and the other one was arrested."

"Thank goodness. I'm sorry your mom has to watch the kids. I know what a chore that is for her."

"It's no chore. My mom is in seventh heaven. She loves having them with her. They are all staying at my place while your house is being taken care of. I don't want you worrying about them. They are having a ball playing football on the beach with Angel and me."

"How long do you think I have to stay here?" I asked Angel as he was changing the dressing on my wound.

"You will be here a few more days. Your foot isn't broken, but it's swollen and bruised. How did that happen?"

"That guy held it in place so he could slam it with the door of his truck. I tried getting away from him, but I was vomiting because he hit my head with that steel bar. I have to admit, I was glad I made a mess in his truck."

"I'm glad you did, too." I looked at Kash when he said that. "I have something for you." He opened his hand, and a pair of hearing aids were in it.

"Oh, where did you get these? I'm going to owe that doctor forever. Thank you." I took them and put them on. It was wonderful. I smiled through my tears.

"You don't owe him anything. They are a gift. I have another surprise for you."

"Another one." I tilted my head and looked at him. "It's not my birthday. What is my other surprise?"

"We found Graham."

I stopped breathing. My head got light, and I thought I would pass out. I held my hand up to my mouth. I had to ask, but I was already crying from the answer. "Is he dead?" I asked between sobs. Kash sat on the bed beside me. He took my hands in his and kissed my dried, cracked lips so softly it was like a feather passed over them.

"No, he's alive."

I started sobbing, and I couldn't stop. The nurse came running into the room. "What is going on in here?"

Angel looked at her. "She just got some great news."

I looked at Kash. "Where is he?"

"He's been held prisoner for three years. Now he's in a hospital because he's run down, but he's fine. The Iranian government claimed to know nothing about him being in prison there. And maybe that's true. Who knows? Ryan and Matt are on their way to get him."

"How did you find him?"

"We know a lot of people."

"I can't believe it. All this time, he's been a prisoner. Why hasn't our government done something? Oh my God, my brother is alive." I cried until he climbed into bed with me and held me.

"Why are you crying?"

I raised my head, and Jason looked like he would start crying at any minute. Poor Jason, he has been through so much. "Jason, Graham is alive."

"What?" Jason felt behind him for a place to sit. "How do you know?"

Kash answered because I was crying so much. "Our team found him. He was in prison in Iran. Ryan and Matt are on their way to bring him back. He won't be the same Graham, you two know. He's been in prison in a hostile country. He wasn't being held where most of the other prisoners were. He was way out in the middle of nowhere. We have some men there that we pay, and they find things for us. This time, they found your brother."

"My brother is alive!" He broke down. Kash moved away from me and went to him. He put his arms around Jason. I loved this man so much. But I had so much baggage. I could never ask him to be with us.

Jason sniffled and Kash gave him the napkins. He blew his nose. "There is so much going on. I'm sorry for acting like a baby. I can't wait to see him."

"As soon as they meet up with him, he'll call you guys. Jason, you are not acting like a baby. You saved your family by fighting two men and being stabbed twice. So, if anyone should break down, it's you. I am so proud of you."

"I'm so proud of you, too." I was still crying, thinking about how to pay Kash back for all he'd done. He saved me from that crazy man. I needed to call the kids. I watched as Kash talked to Jason. He's so good with the kids. My life is so chaotic right now. What is going on with my business? "I need to call all of my clients and let them know what is going on," I spoke out loud without realizing it.

"Everyone knows what's going on. You and Jason are in all the papers because your father's lawyer was arrested and put in jail, as was Maggie's cousin."

"I'm glad their plan failed. Bastards," I said, looking at Kash and Jason. Both of them grinned at me. I smiled. Everything would be alright. I looked at Kash, "How will I ever pay you back?"

"I don't want you to pay me back," he said, smiling. "I'll think of something later," Kash said, winking at me. Jason chuckled.

"Emily, they are releasing me tomorrow. What am I supposed to do?"

"I'll pick you up," Kash said before I could answer. "You'll be staying with me for now. I already have your room ready. If my mom starts trying to baby you and you don't like it, tell me, and I'll talk to her."

"Emily, can I get a dog like Max? He is the best dog. I love him. I remember him jumping through the air past me, knocking that guy over. Then I blacked out. I would love a dog like that."

"I think we can handle that. You can start looking for a dog when you get out." I looked at Kash, "When will Angel let me go home?"

"When you are well enough, then he'll release you. You don't want to go home and end up back in here, do you?"

"No, I don't. Don't you think it's strange the police haven't been here to ask me questions?"

"I think they feel guilty as hell because they had that woman who destroyed all of your calls was dating one of the cousins. She threw your file out, so it was never investigated. So I think they're luckier than hell that you don't sue this whole damn county."

"Don't get upset. I'm sorry I mentioned it."

"They talked to me," Jason said.

Both of us looked at Jason. "Who talked to you?" I asked.

"The police came to my room the day after I was brought to the hospital."

"Do you remember who it was?"

"Yeah, it was the chief. He asked me what had happened. Then he said something stupid."

"What did he say?"

"He asked if my sister was dating either of those men

who came to kill us. I told him my sister would never date anyone like those men."

"What a bastard." They looked at me again and grinned.

"You seem to like that word," Kash said, chuckling.

"It's the only one I can think of right now."

26

EMILY

I WAITED ANXIOUSLY FOR KASH TO PICK ME UP. FINALLY, I GET to go home today. I was dressed and waiting. I looked up, and my brother, Graham, stood in the doorway. I stared at him, then I broke down crying. He hurried over and wrapped me in his arms as we cried together.

"I'm sorry I left you alone to take care of all of this," he said.

"What are you talking about? You were a prisoner of war. You don't have any reason to be sorry. I missed you so much. I tried finding you."

"I know, Jason told me. I'm sorry Dad and Maggie were killed. I'm going to help you with the kids. Besides having bruises all over, you look really nice."

I chuckled and hugged Graham again. "I'm so happy Kash and his buddies found you."

"Me too. Kash is signing you out of here, and then we'll go home. So we live in the house next to Kash?"

"Yes, I rent it. You're staying with us, aren't you?"

"Yes. I'm never leaving my family again."

"What was prison like?"

"I was never mistreated. I think that being held in prison surprised my jailers. They hadn't gotten any paperwork on me. I don't even know why I was being held. But I was always fed and allowed out in the yard. I was the only American there. I had an entire wing of the prison to myself. I read a lot of books. I've actually written a few. When I get my mind together, I'll send them to a publisher or publish them myself. I'm going to take it slow.

Emily, I will help you with everything. I've met the baby. She is so special. She thinks Max belongs to her. She loves Kash. Tell me about you two."

"Yes, tell me about us as well," Kash said, walking into the room with my papers.

I smiled at him and limped to where he stood. "I'm pretty darn close to falling in love. That's all I'm going to say."

He laughed, then he pulled me up against him and kissed me. "I'm pretty close to falling head over heels in love, too." My stomach fluttered. He kissed me again. "Are you ready to go home?"

"Yes, I'm ready."

As soon as I walked into the house, I knew something was up. Then the kids started shouting welcome home. Kelsey ran to me on her little legs, along with the boys. I spread my arms wide and held onto all of them.

"Mommy, home."

I looked at Kelsey. "Yes, sweetheart, Mommy's home." Everyone smiled at me. "It's good to be home."

Marge hugged me. "It's good to have you home. We are having pizza for dinner tonight."

"That sounds yummy."

~

I WATCHED Emily as we sat around with her brothers, eating pizza. Kelsey sat on her lap, and she kept taking Emily's hand and putting it around her. Emily would look at her and tickle her so she could hear Kelsey giggle. She looked at me and smiled as she raised her eyebrows. I smiled back. I loved her. What was I going to do? If Emily and I were to get married, we wouldn't be like most newlyweds who could stay in bed and make love all day. Ours would be after the children were asleep. I had to stop my thoughts right there because my arousal was getting hard and noticeable.

Do I want to have all of these kids living with me? They've lived with me for three weeks already. And I loved having them here with me. Graham could live next door and help when we wanted to be alone. Most married couples go away to be alone. What am I thinking? Am I ready to get married? Would Emily even say yes if I asked her?

"What are you looking at? Do I have pizza sauce on my face?"

I shook my head. I knew I had a serious look on my face. This was very serious to me. I shook myself out of my reflections and joined in the fun talk around the table. Before long,

Kelsey came over and climbed onto my lap. She went to sleep holding my thumb. I swear I felt like I would bawl like a baby just because a two-year-old went to sleep almost every night holding my thumb. I looked at my mom to see what she thought. I knew she knew what I was thinking. The wretched woman had tears running down her cheeks.

"Marge, why are you crying?" Emily asked.

"I'm just so happy. I have never had so much love in my life. Sure, I have my son, but these kids love me. I'm happy, so I'm crying."

I watched the kids looking at her. Then Jason got up and

went to her, hugging her. He kissed her on the cheek, and she patted his hand. That's when it dawned on me that I hadn't been sharing my life with my mother. When Dad was alive, I would go over and talk to him, and then we would have dinner together. Since he died, I had only gone there when Mom asked me to come over. Things are going to change. Since meeting Emily and the kids, I've changed. The new me is a nicer person to be around.

"Did Angel go back to his island?"

I looked at Emily as she waited for my answer. "Yes, he said he needed to make more whiskey. I don't know why he calls it whiskey. It's more like white lightning. It's the strongest drink I have ever tasted."

Emily looked at me and smiled. Then she looked around. I knew she was ready to go home but didn't want to. "Emily, why don't you guys stay here with Mom and me tonight? If you feel better tomorrow, you can go home then. Kelsey is so used to sleeping with her Grammy, Marge. What do you say?"

"That's so kind of you, but you have done so much for us. I feel like I'm taking advantage of you."

"That's crazy. You are not taking advantage of Mom or me. We want to be taken advantage of. Isn't that right, Mom?"

"Yes, I would word it differently, but I love being here with the kids. I feel so much younger. I run on the beach, and we play basketball. We all swim together. Kelsey is becoming an outstanding swimmer."

"Thank you, I know what you mean. I've lost weight playing with the kids. They do make you feel younger."

"Then it's settled."

"I think I'm going to head back over next door. I'm so

used to going to sleep so early. It'll be a while before I change that habit," Graham said, standing up.

Jason stood up. "I'll go over with you, Graham. I'll see all of you in the morning."

I could tell Emily was torn between staying and going. I knew she wanted to stay with me but wanted to be with Graham and Jason, too.

I handed a sleeping Kelsey to Jason and took Emily's hand in mine. "Emily, do you love me?"

"Why are you asking me that? Kash, do you love me?"

"Yes."

"You do?"

"Yes, I do."

"Why? I'm a mess. Look at me. I'm not like the women you date. I'm more comfortable in a kitchen than anywhere else. I don't drink cocktails. I drink sweet tea."

"I haven't been with anyone except for you in the last year." I saw her face turn pink. "I asked you a question. Do you love me?"

"Yes, I love you. Now tell me why you had to ask that question in front of our family."

"Because I wanted them to know you and the children will be staying here with me every night. You know Max will never let the kids out of his sight anymore. He follows Jason around like he's his baby. He sleeps in my mom's bed with her and Kelsey. All of you belong to me. I love every one of you. Can we see where this will go? Could you stay here with me? I don't want you ever to be away from me."

Emily wiped a tear from her cheek. "Yes, I can stay here, and we will see if we work well together."

"Good." I pulled her into my arms and kissed her. I didn't let go for a long time. "Let's get your things." I looked at Jason. "You can give Kelsey to Grammy."

"I'll still have to cook on my big stove, so I'll keep the house. Graham will stay there. She looked over at Jason. "Are you going to be okay sleeping in the house?"

"Yes, I've been sleeping there already. Plus, Graham is there, and I'm getting myself a dog. Kash is getting one for me."

"Okay, but you know we eat together as a family. Breakfast and dinner."

"I know, I wouldn't want to eat anywhere else. I have my grammy and all of my family. Where else would I want to eat."

If I asked Emily to marry me, I knew she would say no because she thought she had too much baggage. But by asking her to be with me, I got her to agree, and once they were all so used to being with me, the next thing to do would be to get married. She'll have to say yes. So until that time comes, we will spend our lives together and never be apart. I love the noise the kids make. It's the noise of life, and I can't wait for more kids and more noise. I have found the love of my life, and I love all the baggage that comes with her.

THE END

If you would like a bonus story about Kash and Emily, here is your link. You'll need to sign up for my NewsLetter.

HTTPS://BOOKHIP.COM/JWFBPHW

Dear reader.

Thank you, for your continued support. I really appreciate that you read my books.

If you can please leave me a review for this book, I would appreciate it enormously.

Your reviews allow me to get validation I need to keep going as an Indie author.

Just a moment of your time is all that is needed. I will try my best to give you the

best books I can write.

BOOK TWO
ANGEL
My Book

Keep reading for book two in my ARMY RANGERS SPECIAL OPS: ANGEL.

27

ANGEL

I LIVE ON HALF OF AN ISLAND. I DON'T KNOW IF ANYONE LIVES on the other half. I've never checked the cabin there to see if anyone came to the island. I live a simple life in my six-room cabin. I enjoy my own company probably more than most people. I don't mind the company of my Army Ranger buddies. I enjoy women, but I would never bring one here to my island. This is my sanctuary.

Every once in a while, one of my buddies will come by and stay a few days with me. I try not to think about the wars I've been in or my friends who have been blown up. I was a surgeon in the Army Ranger Special Forces. I've put men together as best I could when they stepped on mines. I want those pictures out of my head. Sometimes my thoughts would drive me crazy. That's why I used to drink myself to sleep every night. I don't do that anymore. I stopped making my own whiskey. Kash said it would kill me. It was the most potent poison he had ever drunk. I told him that way; you only needed a little to put you to sleep.

I dove under the waves one last time. Tomorrow I'll be leaving my island. I'll miss all the quiet. I have a list of new books I will bring back next month. That's what having half of an island was all about. You have your very own vacation spot. But I also loved my home in Maine. My beach house was down the road from my buddy Kash Walker's. He was getting married in three days, and I was his best man. I knew Kash would lecture me if I didn't get there on time. He and Emily have lived together for a year, and he finally convinced her to marry him.

I was stretched out on the sand when I heard someone shouting for help. *What the hell*? I was on this island alone, at least I thought I was. I jumped up and looked around. A girl about thirteen or so came running from the enemy's side of the island. Thank God I had my swimming trunks on since I usually walked around here in my birthday suit. I couldn't believe there was someone on the other side of the Island. I have never seen anyone there before.

"Hey, what's going on." I watched as a cute girl with red hair flying out behind her stop and looked at me before she continued to walk toward me. "Where did you come from?"

"I'm from the other side of the island. I know you are my enemy, but my aunt fell through a hole in the roof of our house yesterday, and she can't get out of bed. I hope you're not a killer. I don't know why we are enemies, but I should warn you I have a black belt in martial arts, and my kick could knock your head off."

"I'll remember that. Shouldn't we hurry and check on your aunt?"

"Yes. Have you ever been to our side of the mountain?"

"No, my enemy lives on that side. Okay, I have to admit I've jogged around the island and ran past your side. But I've never stopped and looked inside the cabin."

"Why are we enemies?"

"I was never told the reason. I'll tell you what. Starting right now, you and I are no longer enemies."

"My great-grandma said you have horns. I can tell by looking at you that she was kidding me. I don't see one horn."

Angel laughed, "What's your name?"

"Madelaine, everyone calls me Maddie."

"Maddie, my grandma's name was Madelaine."

"My great-great grandma's name was Madelaine."

"My name is Angel. I think we have just figured out why there was a feud between our great-grandfathers. So, this is what your side of the island looks like," I said as we reached their side. It was run down as if it had been abandoned like there hadn't been anyone there for years. So that's why it looks like this. I would have known if they had been coming here.

"Yeah, my aunt owns it now. No one has been here for years. Ainsley is going to fix it up."

I hoped the damn place didn't fall on my head when I walked inside. The place was an old two-room shack. This must be the same cabin built when the island was bought. Why hasn't anyone been back here? It's a beautiful island. I guess they were still thinking of the feud.

"Aunt Ainsley, I'm back. I'll check and see if it's okay if you go in there," Maddie said, walking into the other room. Auntie, he so gorgeous; let's fix your hair, Maddie whispered, trying to calm down Ainsley's wild mane of auburn hair.

"Maddie, honey, I don't care what my hair looks like. I need help to get off of this island. I'm sorry we have to cut our trip short. We'll come back. On your next trip home, I promise. Now please send him in here so I can get out of this bed. The first thing to go will be this damn bed."

Maddie came to the door and motioned me over. I looked up to see an enormous hole in the roof. Then I looked at the bed. My eyes took her all in at once. Her beautiful auburn hair was in all directions, her eyes were a dark blue, and she was sunburned. I could tell she was in a lot of pain. She was looking me over as well. "Hello, I'm Angel Davis."

"Angel Davis, excuse me, my name is Ainsley Davis."

"She means Ainsley Scott."

"What did I say?"

"Auntie, you said, Ainsley Davis. As you can see, she needs help."

"Where do you hurt?" Her voice set me on fire. How could someone have that sexy of a voice? It made me want to take a drink of Tennessee whiskey, then kiss her long and hard. I had to step back because I wanted to lock my lips onto hers. That's when I realized she was talking.

"I thought it was my arm and head, but I must have fallen asleep right after I fell because I went to sleep without remembering going to bed. It was almost dark anyway. And I can't get out of bed. Can you please take us to the mainland?"

"Do you mind if I check you first? I'm a doctor. You'll have to go to the hospital for x-rays. I can see if anything is broken."

"Really."

I almost laughed at the look that came over her face. Her eyes narrowed, and she looked at me like I was crazy. After all, I had swimming trunks on and nothing else. Then she had a scared look as she looked at Maddie. "Let's see if we can get you out of bed. That way, we'll see if you can stand on your own. I'm glad I decided to do another dive before I left. I'm leaving the island today also. My buddy is getting married, and I'm his best man. Emily insists I'm there for the wedding dinner.

"Okay."

I helped her to pull the covers back and saw the bruises.

"Auntie, look at your poor body," Maddie exclaimed. Then she started crying.

"Maddie, sweetie, it's alright the bruises will go away. Don't worry about it. The doctor here will help me up, and then he'll take us with him. When we have enough bars for you to use your phone, you can call your father and tell him to pick us up."

I got in front of Ainsley and inhaled her scent. She smelled like strawberries and vanilla. I saw her grimace as we tried standing her up. "Look, Ainsley, I want you to lie back down. I have to check you for broken bones. If nothing is broken, you should be fine in a few days. What did you hit your head on?"

"My suitcase."

I looked over at her suitcase and saw that it was hard plastic. I first looked at her head, there was a large bump, but it didn't crack her skull. I checked her arms. The right wrist was sprained. "I'll make you something so your arm won't hurt as much." I started on her legs. She had on a pair of short shorts. Damn, I could feel my erection growing and was glad I had on my baggy swim trunks. Her legs were gorgeous. I went as fast as I could. So, she wouldn't think I enjoyed touching her legs, which I did. "Does your back hurt?"

"I hurt everywhere, but I think it's more of the fall bruising my body. It was such a shock one minute I was walking, and the next, I was a crumpled heap on the floor. I'm surprised the floor didn't cave in. This place needs a lot of work. I think I need to hire someone."

"I think we need to go over to my place. Maddie, do you need to pack anything? I'll carry your aunt over to my home."

"What, no you can't carry me to your house. I'm too heavy. It's on the other side of the island."

I acted as if she hurt me. I held my hand to my heart and moaned. "Oh, you stabbed me with a knife right through my heart. Do I look like a weakling that can't carry you to the other side of the island? It's not that far."

"I need to get my things together." She sighed and called her niece over to her. "Can you please pack my electronic stuff in my small carry bag? Heck, I don't even know why I brought it. It's not like I can use it here. We have no electricity. Can you put my purse in your bag? The rest of my items can stay here. I'll have someone come out and fix the roof. We'll put in some solar panels."

"Yes, I'll have it all packed in no time. This is so exciting. I can't wait to come back. I go away to school in two weeks so it will probably be when I have my break. At least we had a week here. I'm almost finished packing already."

I picked Ainsley up, and she fitted perfectly in my arms. We were halfway there when Maddie caught up to us.

"How do you feel, Auntie?"

"I feel like I was thrown from an airplane and landed on top of some pine trees. I'm sorry to have brought you into my troubles," Ainsley said, looking at me.

"Don't worry about it. So where do you go to school, Maddie?"

"Paris. My mother lives in Paris. I live at the boarding school. But when I'm out of school, I stay with my dad. He lives in Tampa, where Ainsley lives. My grandparents live there too. When I'm eighteen, I'll live with them. I'm going to college in Florida."

"I'm sure the doctor doesn't want to hear about everyone in our family, sweetie."

"I don't mind. I enjoy listening to stories about families. I no longer have any family. I guess that's why I'm always at my friend Kash's house. His fiancé is raising her five young siblings. So, their home is always so exciting and noisy. Emily is a chef, so there are always tons of food. They're getting married in three days."

"What do you do?" I Knew before she asked, she was going to try a trick question on me.

"I'm a doctor—some of the times. Plus, I also rescue people who are stuck in other countries. I don't have just one job I do. I would rather have an option on what I want to do."

"Wow, that sounds exciting. Are you able to rescue very many people?"

"If we're lucky, we can. It all depends if they can hide long enough before they are found. Whatever you hear on the news is all lies. The people are trying to leave, but the Taliban won't let them go. They are starving them to death. There are Americans over there dying, and our government ignores them. I'm sorry, I have a lot of issues with Afghanistan and a few other countries."

Maddie patted me on the back. "There is nothing wrong with that. I'm sure if everyone knew what was going on, they would all become angry."

"How old are you?"

"I'm fourteen, and I watch the news a lot. I'm going to be a journalist."

"My friend might discourage you on that. She says it gets in her blood, and she needs to be in those dangerous places. So people can see what is really going on. Lara is a war reporter."

"Are you talking about Lara West?"

"Yes, do you know her?"

She was almost jumping up and down with her excitement. I was glad it got her aunt's mind off me carrying her. "I wish I knew her. She is my idol. I love her."

"I'll tell her what you said. She's the bridesmaid."

"Oh wow. Do you think you could get Lara's autograph for me?"

"I'm sure I can. Give me your address, and one of us will mail it to you." I stopped when I heard Ainsley gasp.

"Oh my, this is your side of the island. Why did you get the good side? Are you sure you took the right side?" She chuckled.

"I believe this has always been our side. My grandfather built his home around my great-grandfathers. I'll show it to you, he went to pick her up again, but Ainsley stopped him. "I'll take your arm. You can help me by letting me hang on to you. You've carried me enough."

We walked inside, and Ainsley stopped and looked at the old cabin inside the new one. "It's fabulous. I love it. Your grandfather had an artist's mind. This place is fantastic. Did these old quilts belong to your great-grandmother? They make great wall hangings. I'm so jealous."

"You're welcome to come here whenever you want. Bring Maddie with you. We have an entire library inside of the old cabin. I leave the key under the pot in the front."

"That's very kind of you. Do you know why our great grandfathers were enemies? I mean, they were best friends." Ainsley didn't tell him she knew the reason.

"No, when Maddie and I talked, she told me she was named after her great-great-grandmother. My grandma's name was Madelaine. I believe something was going on between your great-grandmother and my great-grandfather."

"Wow, that might be true, because when they left here, they never came back. They moved to New York, and that's where they stayed. My great-grandfather started building homes, and my brother is still building houses. My grandparents moved to Tampa."

28

AINSLEY

I can't breathe. If he backs away, I know I'll breathe again. My God, I didn't expect my neighbor to look like Adonis. I could melt in his eyes. He was so handsome. I think I lost my heart to him before he picked me up. But after he picked me up, my God, his smell, I almost licked his neck. That would have shocked the heck out of him. He smelled so good. *Ainsley, stop it, for Pete's sake.* You do not go around licking people for crying out loud. And you aren't going to start now. Just because he's hot and dreamy and a doctor and rescues people doesn't mean you lost your heart. I tried calming my hair. I felt like bawling my head off. I thought the guy was old; I didn't even think to fix my hair. I should have known something when Maddie came in and tried to make me look better.

I watched as he ran around his home doing things to lock it up again. Then he brought Maddie and me a sandwich and a glass of ice tea. I couldn't keep my eyes off of him. He sat down to eat his food, and he smiled at me. My heart melted again.

"Is this the first time you've been to the island?"

When I realized he was talking to me, I had to shake myself. "Yes, I had heard we had half of an island. But no one had ever been to it. When my uncle died, he left it to me. Maddie and I thought we would start using it."

"Do you see Maddie often?"

"We fly over to her school as much as we can. We stay at the hotel until she has to go back." I knew he was curious about Maddie's school. But he was polite enough not to ask anything personal.

"I stay at a boarding school. My mother is too busy to have me with her."

"That's too bad."

"Yeah, I wish I could live here with my family. I miss them not being with me. I'm not too fond of boarding school. I have two friends there who I like. But they always go home on the weekends."

The entire time Maddie talked; I watched Angel. He looked up a few times as we ate our food. "Thank you for lunch. It was delicious."

"Yes, thank you," Maddie said.

"You're welcome. I'll finish locking up my home, and then I'll load the boat, and we'll leave."

"Okay, thank you." I looked over at Maddie, and mouthed 'oh my God, I love him.' Maddie giggled and covered her face up. She hurried over and sat right next to me. "Did you see those dimples?" She giggled again.

"I think his eyes are pretty too. Did you see all of his muscles?"

"Did I see them?" I whispered. "He carried me all the way over here from our cabin, and he was shirtless." I raised my eyes as I saw him walking down the stairs. He was dressed in jeans that hung low on his hips and a button-up blue dress shirt. "I feel underdressed." I looked down at my shorts and tee shirt.

"You look beautiful." He said, watching me.

"Thank you."

"Are we ready to go down to the boat?"

"Yes. I will walk and hold on to your arm."

"Aww, I was looking forward to carrying you." I wish I would have let him carry me by the time we went ten feet; my foot was killing me. "I'm sorry, but I believe you will have to carry me."

He put one arm around me and his other arm under my knees, and he lifted me like I weighed nothing. I even laid my head on his shoulder. I knew I could become very attached to Angel Davis. His boat was beautiful. Plus, it had lots of room.

The only problem was that the ride was over way too fast. He had his own boat slip. After Maggie and he tied it off. He took out our bags. I only had my carrying bag, and Maddie had her small suitcase. Angel had a duffel bag. We were unloaded, and after he put me on the dock, I saw my brother walking toward us.

"What the hell happened to you. My God, your entire body is bruised."

"Yes, it is. James, this is Angel Davis. He saved our lives. Angel, this is my brother and Maddie's father, James Scott." At least James finally realized he had manners. "Damn, thank you. He pulled Maddie to him and hugged her. So, you are the enemy. I've heard that story, but I don't know what caused it. Do you happen to know the entire story?"

I saw Angel's dimples and smiled. He looked at Maddie. She watched Angel. He winked at her and wiggled his eyebrows. "No, I don't know the story, but Maddie and I figured out that she and my grandma had the same name."

"Just what I suspected all along, there was some fooling around going on way back then. Your great-grandfather was single when they lived here. Hey, thanks for rescuing these two."

"I always wanted to meet my neighbor, and now I have two new friends. Ainsley needs x-rays. Bye, Ainsley. It was a pleasure meeting you. Maddie, I can't wait to see you again."

"Bye, Angel, don't forget Lara West's autograph."

"I won't forget." He looked at James. "You'll have to carry Ainsley. She has a badly sprained ankle."

I didn't want him to leave. I wanted him to carry me. I felt like I was getting desperate, but I didn't want him to go. *What should I do?*

"My dad has a bad back; I'm sure he won't be able to carry Ainsley." I looked at Maddie and smiled. James was about to say something. I interrupted him. "I'm sure I can walk," I said weakly.

"No, I'll carry you." Angel picked me up and carried me to James's truck. He sat me in the back seat. Then he looked at me. "You take care of yourself," he said as he went to turn back around.

Angel," I said. He turned around and faced me. "Thank you for everything." I leaned out, took his face in my hands, and kissed him. I decided right then I was taking the lead. Why should a woman wait for the man to take control? Angel took over. He pulled me gently toward him and deepened the kiss. When he raised his head, we both smiled.

"Let me see your phone."

I handed my phone to him and watched as he entered his phone number into my phone. "Now you have my phone number. Call me." "I watched him walk away.

"Did you just kiss a stranger that you've only known a few hours?"

"Yes, I did."

"Yes! Way to go, Aunt Ainsley.

"Why did you kiss him?"

"Because I lost my heart to him, and I couldn't help myself."

"We need to get you an x-ray for your head."

"Dad, he's perfect for Aunt Ainsley." I looked at father and daughter. "I don't want to go back to that school. I want to be with my family. Since I told mom I wanted to live with you, I haven't seen her. That's been six months. She never visits me. My friends go home for weekends, I don't even get a call from her. Please try harder to make her let me live with my family."

"I will, sweetheart. I've been talking to a few people. It won't be long now. I promise, you will be living with us soon. I am speaking to a judge next week. I'll know something then. You have one more week to be with us. Why don't you and I go to Disney world?"

"I would love to go to Disney World with you, Daddy."

"Can we get my tired body x-rayed first?" I said, making both of them laugh. I worried about Maddie being in that boarding school all alone. Kids weren't supposed to be away from their families. *I'll go up there more often and be with her.* We pulled into the hospital emergency, and there was a wheelchair waiting for me. The nurse pushed me straight to the x-ray room.

"Wow, I didn't know I could be taken care of this fast."

"Doctor Angel asked us to take care of you. He's so hot who could tell him no."

I chuckled. "I know, right. When he examined my legs and arms, I could have fainted, and wouldn't you know my hair looks like a tornado got a hold of it. I like calling him

Doctor Angel, now whenever I think of him, that's what I will remember."

"We used to call him Doctor Hotty, but one of the nurses messed up and called him that over the speaker when he came in to help out with a patient."

I chuckled because I could understand how she could slip up like that."

"Your voice sounds so familiar."

"That's because I'm on the radio." I used my sexy radio voice. "This is late night with Doctor Ainsley. Tell me what your problem is."

"Oh, wow. I listen to you all the time. I was going to call you like a hundred times. Are you a doctor?"

"I'm a psychologist."

"Wow, you get some scary crazies on your calls. Do they scare you?"

"They used to. I have security now—two big burly guys who walk me to my car."

"That's good. How did you get all of these bruises?"

"I was checking out my roof on an old cabin that my uncle left me. I thought I saw some light coming through a crack. I climbed on the roof and fell through it."

"You poor thing. I'll leave you here, and the x-ray tech will take you in. I'll wait here for you."

"Thank you." I was in there and out of there quickly. My foot was severely sprained, and two of the tiny bones on top of my foot were broken. My wrist was also sprained. The knot on the back of my head was better. The doctor said I had a concussion.

It's such a strange feeling. I feel like I miss doctor Angel already. I must be having effects from the medication I took. I sighed as I sat in the back seat of James's truck. I was so dang tired. I decided when I got home; I would sleep for two days. But when I got home, that didn't happen. All of my aunts and Uncles were there, plus my cousins. "James, I can't visit anyone right now. Would you please drive me to my place? I know it's close, but I can't walk."

"Let's say hello, then I'll take you home."

"Can you see what I'm wearing, I'm in the same clothes I had on yesterday, and I also slept in them. My body is covered in bruises, for Pete's sake. I had a concussion, and it knocked me out. It's going to be bad enough when mom sees me. Are grandma and grandpa here as well. I can't see them either. Grandpa will want me to stay away from that place. I'm begging you."

"Say hello, then we will leave."

"I wasn't happy with his answer, but Maddie had already gone inside, and my mother and father were coming out to meet us.

"Oh, Ainsley, sweetie, you poor thing. Why would you get on the roof for crying out loud?"

"Mom, I could see some light coming from my ceiling in the bedroom. What was I supposed to do? I couldn't ignore it, for Pete's sake. I've grown up helping dad, and I wouldn't let my roof go unfixed."

"Sweetheart, you fell off the roof."

"No, Mom, I'm not that clumsy. I fell through the roof. There is a big difference. I can't visit right now; I need to take a long soak in the tub."

"They came to see you. Say hello, and then you can go to your wing."

Mom called our homes wings because our homes were all on the same property, and they were angled in a way that looked like wings. I saw my sister running to us. I would plead with Harper to save me from our family.

"Oh, my God, look at you. Mom, Ainsley cannot go in

there. She's a mess. The gossip would be circling in no time. They would have Ainsley drunk on the roof and fell off of it by the time the buzz stopped talking about her. Nope, she can't go in there. James drive around to her place. I'll tell everyone that she took a muscle relaxer and went to sleep. They just want to say the island is a horrible place.

Our dad looked at Harper. "Harper, how come you can always come up with an easy lie to tell. When did you start telling lies?"

I chuckled, as did the rest of them. Harper could talk her way out of anything since she was three years old. She didn't tell lies, at least not lies that would hurt anyone. But she knew just what to say. She jumped in the vehicle with us and talked all the way there. As soon as James carried me inside, she started my bathwater. She put a ton of bath salts in it and then turned toward me. "You can tell me all about Angel while you soak."

"Maddie didn't waste time in telling you about Angel Davis. Can you help me get this top off, please?"

"Dang, girl, there isn't a spot on you that isn't bruised. I'm sure you can't get that wet cast in the water. I'll get something for you to prop it up. Damn, your entire ass is bruised. For crying out loud, you could've been killed. Grandpa said that place was haunted. That's why he would never go there."

"How could it be haunted if no one died there?"

"Maybe someone died before the ancestors moved there. Did you see anything of our enemy there?"

"Didn't Maddie tell you? Our enemy is Doctor Dreamy. He carried me to his side of the island. His home there is fantastic. I lost my heart the moment I looked into his eyes. He is so gorgeous. He's a doctor, on the side, He's a retired Army Ranger (Special Ops,) he rescues people overseas that got left behind. He goes into those countries where they have to hide to survive."

"What is his name? I'm going to look him up."

"Use my laptop and bring it in here. His name is Angel Davis. When I introduced myself, I said hi, I'm Ainsley Davis." I watched my sister almost pee herself laughing. "Then Maddie said no, your name is Ainsley Scott."

"Oh my God, I would have given anything to have been there and listened to you talking. Ainsley Davis, that's too much."

"Just look him up. I want to see his face again." I closed my eyes then I slipped under the water. When I raised up, I reached for the shampoo, but I had to wait for Harper to get back. I couldn't reach that far. "Can you hand me the shampoo?" While she looked Angel up on the computer, I shampooed my hair. "I kissed him before he left."

Harper raised her head and stared at me like I was crazy. You kissed a stranger?"

"I couldn't help myself."

"Oh lord, I've lost my heart as well."

"No, you don't. He's mine."

"You didn't tell me he wore glasses."

"Let me see who you are looking at. That's not Angel," I pointed my finger, "there he is. Read to me what it says."

"Doctor Angel Davis worked on the front line, saving many lives and patching up those men who were injured the worst. He was awarded the medal of honor for bravery for going into a burning building and carrying out six men from his team. You're right. He is dreamy. The other one is Ryan Grant. He looks like Clark Kent. I have to say I love superman."

"Let me help you get out of there. Don't try and take a

bath unless I'm here with you. I'm staying here for a few nights until you feel better."

"Thank you, have I told you how lucky I am to have you for a sister?"

"You have, but I like to hear it often." I chuckled as Harper helped me to bed.

JOIN me on social media Follow me on BookBub
https://www.bookbub.com/profile/susie-mciver

NEWSLETTER   SIGN   UP   HTTP://BIT.LY/
SUSIEMCIVER_NEWSLETTER

FACEBOOK PAGE: www.facebook.com/SusieMcIverAuthor/

FACEBOOK   GROUP: www.facebook.com/
groups/SusieMcIverAuthor/

HTTPS://WWW.SUSIEMCIVER.COM/

MORE BOOKS by Susie McIver

KILLIAN BOOK 1
    My Book

. . .

ROWAN BOOK 2
<u>My Book</u>

ZANE BOOK 3
<u>My Book</u>

STORM BOOK 4
<u>My Book</u>
ASH BOOK 5
<u>My Book</u>

JONAH BOOK 6
<u>My Book</u>

KANE BOOK 7
My Book

AUSTIN BOOK 8
My Book
LUKE BOOK 9
My Book
RYES BOOK 10
My Book